SOME LOVES NEVER DIE

Monsters and Mayhem Book Four

E A COMISKEY

To Chris Wilson, for naming Stan Kapcheck. Just the name I needed for the character in my head.

TRADEMARK ACKNOWLEDGEMENTS

Volkswagen Beetle
Northface
Mack Truck
The Little Engine that Could
Jack in the Box

CHAPTER ONE

Richard

OUTSIDE THE STORYBOOK CABIN SNUGGLED AWAY IN THE Sangre de Cristo mountains near Santa Fe, New Mexico, fat snowflakes drifted down from heavy gray clouds like the feathers of falling angels. Inside, a fire crackled and popped and saturated the air with fragrant heat.

Richard dipped a tarnished silver spoon into his bowl of green chili stew and came up with a thick chunk of pork and a good amount of broth. On that cold winter day, the flavors burst across his tongue the way the warm desert sun bursts across the mesa in June. He understood the importance of cherishing the best moments of being human. After all, if he'd learned anything in the year since he became a hunter of supernatural evil, it was that death was the least of a man's worries. Death came for everyone. It was only natural. When unnatural things happened to you, *that's* when you needed to worry.

To Richard's left at the table, sat his granddaughter, Burke. She tore off a bit of a homemade flour tortilla and popped it into her mouth before tearing another small piece. She was worried about Greg, her idiot ex-husband, and she was right to be worried. At the moment, however, her big brown eyes were focused on Stan Kapcheck.

Everyone's eyes were always on friggin' Stan Kapcheck, with his stylish leather boots and his well-pressed flannel shirt. What kind of a weirdo took an iron to flannel, anyway?

Richard's eyes burned. He blinked hard. Dang, if he wasn't just as happy as a tornado in a trailer park to have that annoying old peacock whole and healthy again. They'd come all too close to losing Stanley in recent times, and Richard couldn't quite wrap his mind around the idea of life without him, even if he was sometimes as annoying as a mosquito in your underpants.

Stanley sat to Richard's right. He studied the map of the Santa Fe area that lay in the center of the rustic wooden table. "So, we know that Greg was headed for Tesuque, which is due north of town, off of eighty-four, but you say you have it on good authority that he was seen southwest of here, in Agua Fria."

Their host, Nathanial, occupied the final chair at the table, directly across from Richard. Nathanial scratched his bushy, chest-length beard, knocking one of the pink plastic butterfly clips lodged among his whiskers askew. "Not only Agua Fria. He touched base in Chupadero, Cañada de los Alamos, Las Dos—all the way south to Clines Corners. He found ins with the communities, and I mean all of them—the Wiccans, the natives, the Catholics. He spent three days at that nudist spa downtown."

Burke snorted.

Richard scowled. Thinking about his granddaughter's ex-husband with his junk hanging out was enough to kill a healthy man's appetite.

Almost.

Richard scooted his chair back and went to the wood-burning stove to help himself to seconds.

"He wasn't hard to track at first," Nathanial said. "I cast a simple spell and there he was. Then, bam!"

Richard jumped and almost slopped his stew on the floor. He kept his words to himself, though. It didn't seem polite to scold the hand that fed you.

"Bam, what?" Burke asked.

"Bam, he disappeared. He was there. Then he wasn't," Nathaniel said.

Nathanial's cat, Jeremiah, leaped onto his owner's immense lap and helped himself to a few licks of the man's stew.

"Once I lost him, I widened the search to all New Mexico, North America, the world," Nathaniel continued. "Now, y'all know that the wider it goes, the less accurate it gets, but still... there should have been something."

Burke pushed her food aside, half-eaten. "So, he's dead?"

Stanley ran a hand over his shiny bald head. "Not necessarily. Nathanial, you told us earlier that there was a disturbance of some sort, right about the time Greg disappeared. Do you think there's a connection?"

"Sure, I don't know," the big man answered while scratching his cat's head. "I know two things happened. Don't know if they're connected."

"What kind of disturbance? I ain't real clear on what you meant by that," Richard said around a mouthful of green chilis, as he returned to his seat.

"The kind that makes magical folk wake up in the night, sick to their stomach. Something's off. Bad mojo. Energy gone wrong. Poor feng shui. Does that make it clearer?" Nathaniel asked.

"'Bout as clear as barnwood," Richard grumbled.

Burke tapped her nails against the table. The cat watched the dance of pink enameled surfaces with a twitching tail. A loud crack from the fire shifted the logs, sending a volcano of red sparks up the chimney.

"I bedded an aboriginal dream walker once," Nathanial said.

They all stared at him, even the cat.

Nathanial shrugged a ham-hock of a shoulder. "I only bring it up because the poor woman turned out to be as crazy as a loon. She ended up being taken into state custody and, so far as I know, she continues to live out her days weaving macramé under close supervision."

"I'm sure it wasn't your fault," Stanley said.

Richard shook his head and ate his soup. A year earlier, he'd been wasting away at Everest Senior Living, hanging around waiting for Death to come calling as it did for men his age. Turns out he didn't die there. Stanley saved his wrinkled old butt from soul-eating monsters pretending to be nurses, and in the months since, Richard had crisscrossed the lower forty-eight and seen more weird than most people ever dreamed of. That said, the humans out-weirded the monsters on a consistent basis.

"It might have been my fault." Nathanial sounded fairly unconcerned with the idea of driving a woman to madness. "I only bring it up because I think that's where you should start."

Burke's fingers stilled. "With your ex-lover?"

Great, rolling guffaws bellowed from Nathanial. He slapped the table, sending the cat racing for safety in some quieter part of the house. "No, no. She wouldn't be able to tell you anything useful unless your man is in another plane of existence."

"He's *not* my man," Burke said through gritted teeth.

Nathanial went on as though she hadn't spoken. "I think your best lead is Kenneth. He's an orderly at the Villa Cierto Health Care Center for Seniors. He's *special*."

Stanley polished off his dinner and dabbed at the corners of his mouth with a paper napkin. "Would you mind terribly being a bit more specific?"

"Okay," Nathaniel replied.

Burke met Richard's gaze and rolled her eyes. He felt her pain. Listening to the other two men was like trying to make sense out of squirrel chatter.

"About the current topic of conversation, please," Stanley said.

Nathaniel nodded. "Oh, sure. Kenneth is from the Acoma

Pueblo. He wears a lot of turquoise jewelry. He's employed as an orderly, but his real job is keeping the spirits quiet. He's successful more often than not."

Richard leaned forward. "What spirits?"

"All the spirits," Nathanial said.

"In the world?" Burke asked.

Laughter returned—a rolling earthquake of merriment. "Oh, no. No, no, no. That's funny!" Nathaniel waved a hand the size of a dinner plate in front of his whiskered face, then slapped his knee several times in quick succession. After a few deep breaths he said, "Villa Cierto is haunted, of course. It was built on the site of the former graveyard used by the penitentiary and it—"

Richard nearly spit his dentures out. "What in the Sam Hill was any fool thinking, building a dang nursing home on top of a graveyard?"

"The land was inexpensive, I imagine," Nathanial said.

"My God, it must be the most haunted building in the Southwest," Burke said.

Nathanial snorted. "You serious? You haven't spent much time in Santa Fe, have you? Anyway, Villa Cierto ain't so bad. Good old Kenneth keeps things in check."

"And you believe he would know where Greg is?" Stanley asked.

Nathaniel shrugged. "He's as good a guy as any to ask. He's got more eyes in this town than a seraph, and he knows people who know magic far beyond my own."

"By eyes, do you mean monsters?" Burke asked.

"Just people, so far as I know," Nathanial replied.

"You got some pretty good magic," Richard said, thinking of the marvelous healing balm the strange man had given them. The smelly stuff had been a literal lifesaver in the past, not only soothing aching bones and joints, but healing a stab wound to Stanley's heart with miraculous speed.

Nathanial stood and began clearing their plates. "My magic is just parlor tricks, compared to some."

Burke tugged the map toward her side of the table. "Okay. So, tomorrow morning we go into town and talk to this man, Kenneth." She jerked her thumb in the direction of the window beyond, where a yard light illuminated snow that poured downward in a thick white sheet. "I'd go tonight, but I'm not sure we can get off this mountain in the dark with the snow coming down like it is. We shouldn't waste time, though. If Greg's off the grid in a spiritual sense...I mean...that could mean anything, right? It could be like what happened to Stanley or me."

Richard shuddered. It had been a rough few months. Burke's mother had set her up with a loser who ended up sending a demon from a shadow realm to possess Burke and make her obey him. In the rescuing, Stanley lost a piece of himself that left him so wounded they were uncertain he'd recover until only a week or so ago. If his ex-grandson-in-law was in that kind of trouble... well...Burke was right to worry.

"Why do you want so badly to save not-your-man?" Nathanial asked from his place by the sink.

Jeremiah the cat poked his head around the corner as if curious to know the answer to that question.

Burke wrapped her arms around herself. Her gaze wandered from the fireplace, to the rough-hewn beams in the ceiling, and finally landed on Richard. "I was led to this hunt. It's not my place to judge who deserves saving. My job is to stand in the gap between humanity and whatever wants to destroy it."

Pride thumped through Richard's veins with every beat of his feeble old heart. The kid never ceased to amaze him. From her, he was learning what kind of person he wanted to be.

"Very well, then, it's settled," Stanley said. "In the morning, we hunt at the retirement home."

His words brought the reality of the situation sailing into Richard's gut like a well-placed Kung-fu kick. "Hold on."

"Something wrong, Dick?" Stanley asked.

Richard scowled. Lord, but he hated being called Dick and that old fart knew it, too. "You listen to me, Stan Kapcheck. The Devil Herself is gonna be ice skating in Hell before I set foot inside a haunted retirement home." The very thought turned his bowels to water. "I got locked up in a place like that, and I sat there waiting for Death and, by golly, Death darn near found me there."

"Grandpa, you weren't locked up," Burke said.

He smacked his hand on the table. "You don't know how it was. If I never go back in any kind of old folk's home again that'll be too soon, let alone one built on a friggin' prison graveyard."

"You're not scared, are you?" Stanley asked. A grin tipped one corner of his mouth northward.

Burke grasped Richard's hand. "Don't tease, Stanley. Aren't you the one who taught us that wise men listen to their fear, but are never ruled by it? Grandpa will help us. He'll come through. He does, every time."

Richard swallowed the lump in his throat and squeezed the kid's hand. Nathanial stomped over to a shelf, retrieved a fat book, then returned and dropped it on the table.

"What's this?" Burke asked. "A spell book?"

The big man dried his hands on his yellow daisy-print apron. "No, but spelling's important. It's all in alphabetical order. Phone book. Cell service is spotty, at best, in these parts. You might need some good old-fashioned paper sources to find names and addresses." He jerked his hairy chin in Richard's direction. "Maybe he's got a point about the retirement home. Sniff out the trail. See what's to see."

"You could come with us, you know," Stanley said.

Nathanial's eyes grew wide, and he started laughing again. His laughter filled the house. Tears poured out of his eyes and disappeared into the tangle of growth on his face. He shook his head, turned his back, and disappeared down the hall, laughing all the while. A door clicked shut and muffled the sound.

The three hunters of all things supernatural looked at each other.

After a moment, the creak of a door opening reached their ears. "Towels in the closet," Nathaniel called. "Sleep anywhere you like, but not on the big canopy bed. That one's Jeremiah's and he'll claw your eyes out if you lay in it."

The door clicked shut again and they were left to find their own way to their beds.

CHAPTER TWO

Burke

MORNING DIDN'T DAWN OVER SANTA FE THE DAY AFTER THE snowstorm. It exploded. The brilliant sun blazed in a crystal sky where not the tiniest wisp of a cloud remained. The earth, blanketed in ten inches of glittering fresh snow reflected the light back as if trying to outshine the stars.

"Have you guys peeked outside yet this morning?" Burke asked the three men gathered around the kitchen table.

"Beautiful!" Nathanial declared over his full plate.

"A stunning morning," Stanley agreed.

"I ain't been out yet, but by the looks of things I'd say it's colder than a well-digger's butt," her grandfather offered

Burke helped herself to a cup of coffee. She breathed in the aroma of hazelnut and tried to take a sip, but it was too hot, fresh off the burner, and she only succeeded in scalding the tip of her tongue.

Stanley held up a crumpled envelope covered in emerald-green ink. "Nathanial made us a list."

"That's the folks I talked to about your man, or the folks who talked to the folks that I talked to. Or, well, at any rate, that's all the folks I know of who talked to your man," Nathanial said.

Burke sat next to her grandfather and scooted her chair in. "He is *not* my man."

Didn't anyone get it? Her relationship with Greg had been over for years. She'd moved on, met someone else while they'd been on the cruise ship, and he was on his way to be with her, and she was happy about that. Sort of. Maybe. She let the subject drop, and no one said anything more about her love life one way or the other.

"The list goes in order from the people who saw Greg first to those who saw him later, as far as I could piece it together," Nathanial said.

"Okay, who's first?" Burke asked.

Stanley consulted the back of the envelope. "It looks like Greg came in from the north and started contacting people in Chupadero. He worked his way around the outskirts of town in a wide circle, came back through the center, and then north again to Tesuque."

Burke consulted the map on her phone. "None of these places are too terribly far away. Why don't we start with who saw him last and work our way backward as far as need be?"

"That means we talk to Fred Pitts first," Stanley said.

What kind of a sick parent would make a kid go to school with a name like Fred Pitts? Burke tried again to sip her coffee and was rewarded with a second burn.

"What do we know about Fred?" she asked.

Nathanial slopped up the last of the egg yolk on his plate with a slice of toast and stuffed the mess into his mouth. He mopped his face with the edge of his Strawberry Shortcake apron. "Freddie runs a psychic shop and does some stuff for cops and detectives, too. He's the real deal, but he's got a weakness for gambling that keeps him constantly on the down-and-out."

"I'd think a psychic would be a pretty good gambler," Richard said.

Nathaniel nodded. "I'd think so, too, except he's not that kind of psychic. He can't see the future, so far as I've ever heard, and he can't read minds. He reads the past through psychometry. You know; when he touches an object, he gets a feel for where it's been and who else has touched it."

Burke pulled up the map on her phone and traced the route from Nathanial's cabin toward the psychic's house. Jeremiah strolled into the room and leaped onto the big man's lap and received a hearty ear scratching.

"You all be careful out there today, will you?" Nathanial said.

"Aren't we always?" Stanley asked.

Nathanial lifted the cat from his lap, then lowered him to the floor before standing to retrieve his coat from a hook by the door. "No. You're not, and the more I think about that vibe that went out the other day.... I don't know, man. Gives me the willies. Something in the natural order's out of whack."

"Sounds like our cup of tea," Burke said.

"You can make tea out of compost. Don't mean you ought to drink it." With that ominous statement, Nathaniel hefted a bucket of bird seed and went out the front door.

After they finished breakfast, bundled up against the chilly morning and loaded with the variety of guns and knives most frequently used in their particular line of work, Nathanial went out ahead of them and used his over-sized lawn mower with a snowplow attachment to clear a path to the main road. The pavement on the main road was wet but clear, the snow having been pushed to the sides by the county plow trucks. Stanley took a right turn toward town, and Nathanial turned and headed back toward his cabin.

"What's his story, anyway?" Richard asked.

"Nathanial?" Stanley maneuvered around the sharp curve of a hill and shifted the car into second gear to slow their descent. Santa Fe sat at a lofty seven thousand feet above sea level, but many of the houses on the outskirts of town sat on even higher peaks. "His parents were killed when he was just a kid. Hunters saved him and raised him, but he never had it in him to face the monsters himself."

"He's certainly found his own way to help," Burke said from the back seat.

"Indeed, he has," Stanley said. "There aren't many hunters who've passed through this part of the world that don't owe their lives to Nathanial."

Stanley was one of those hunters, and the reminder quieted all of them as they continued to the little village of Tesuque where stunning multi-million dollar homes seemed to grow out of the earth along the rocky hillsides. Smaller houses, some no bigger than shacks, some looking so old they seemed prehistoric, dotted the wide spaces between the mansions.

Among those little dwellings, they found the Pitts' home, a single-story box made out of straw bales with a thick coating of mud spread on the outside. A dog—or was it a coyote—cowered away from them on the end of a chain, under the shelter of a cracked plastic doghouse. The landscaping was pretty much untouched high-desert which meant pokey weeds and hard-baked earth.

An old woman with deep lines around her eyes and limp, stone-gray hair answered their knock by opening the door only as far as the chain would allow.

Burke smiled. "Good morning, Mrs. Pitts. We were wondering if Fred is home and if we could have a word with him."

"He done something wrong?" She turned and shouted into the interior of the house. "Fred, what'd you do? These people are looking for you."

"No, ma'am. He hasn't done anything wrong," Burke hurried to assure her.

"We're looking for a friend of ours who's gone missing. We've got reliable information that Fred spoke with him about a week before he disappeared," Stanley said.

Burke bit her tongue. Greg wasn't her friend, but she supposed that was the easiest way to explain the situation.

"You cops?" the woman asked.

"No, ma'am," Stanley said.

The door slammed shut, and the sound of metal scraping metal reached their ears before the woman opened it again. "Come in, I guess."

Burke led the men into the tiny home. Through one door off the combination living room/kitchen she made out the corner of a bed. Through the second, was a bathroom sink. She guessed, based on the pile of blankets haphazardly folded on one end of the threadbare sofa that Fred Pitts spent his night in his mother's living room.

Fred sat at a round kitchen table covered with a red vinyl cloth. He didn't look up as they approached. His fingers tapped rapidly on the keyboard of a low-budget two-in-one laptop.

"Hold on," he muttered.

The woman slouched off into the bedroom and slammed the door shut. Richard scowled in her direction and Burke sent up a silent prayer that he wouldn't say anything offensive. Fred's fingers slowed then stopped. He glared at each of them in turn.

Burke arranged her face into her best customer service smile. "I'm very sorry to intrude on you like this, Mr. Pitts."

"Mr. Pitts is my father and he's doing twenty in the Supermax," Fred said.

"The movie theater?" Richard asked.

Fred scowled at Richard. "It's the big prison outside of town. You're clearly not from around here."

"Well, we didn't mean to intrude, but we're hoping you can

help us find someone." Burke strained to keep the conversation on track.

"I get paid for that kind of help," Fred said.

Stanley pulled a fifty from his breast pocket as though he'd had it ready for just that moment, and Fred took it without hesitation.

"Who are you looking for?" he asked.

Burke pulled up a picture of Greg on her phone. "This is my ex-husband, Greg. He came in your shop a week or two ago?"

He glanced at the picture for all of two seconds. "Yeah. I remember him."

Stanley explained once again. "He's missing. Is there anything at all you can tell us that you think might help us find him?"

"Do you have anything of his?" he asked.

Burke told him they didn't.

Fred shrugged. "Then there's nothing I can do for you."

"We weren't necessarily looking for psychic help," she said.

"Then what?"

"I'm not sure. Can you tell us anything at all about why he came to you? Did he say anything about where he was going or who he was with? Anything at all out of the ordinary?"

Fred leaned his chair back on the two back legs, and it creaked ominously beneath his bulk. "He Googled and found my name. Knocked on the door without an appointment, just like you. Lots of people seem to think I got nothing to do with my time but sit around and hope they show up."

Stanley returned to his line of questioning, and Burke figured he was avoiding the argument. "Sounds very ordinary," Stanley said. "I'm surprised you remembered him."

"Yeah, well, he was going on about protection stuff. Could I cast a spell to help him avoid bad energy? Stuff like that. I told him I wasn't a witch. He asked if I could see who was after him. I told him I can only see the past. That seemed to turn him off right away. Whatever he did to get himself in trouble, he didn't want me to know about it."

Stanley rocked on his toes. "A man of your unique talents must encounter people like Greg on a fairly regular basis."

Fred picked at something green stuck between his teeth. "Sure. You get some amateur-hour Wiccan chick in here asking for stuff, but this guy was straight as my willy, you get what I'm saying? And he didn't know anything. Like...why's he all worried about black magic when he doesn't even know the difference between quartz and pyrite?"

"Did you ask him why he was so curious?" Burke asked.

"Why would I care?"

Richard huffed. "So you didn't pick up anything at all from him, Carnac?"

"Who's Carnac?"

"Just answer the question," Burke told him. "Before I knock you out of your chair."

He frowned. "Geez lady. Calm your tits. I couldn't read him. Like I said, that's not what I do."

"All right. I think we've learned all we can here. Just one last question. Do you have any idea where Greg might have gone?" Stanley asked.

"Like I said before, why would I care?" He laid his fingers across the keyboard of his laptop and started tapping again. "Mom! They're leaving, can I have some breakfast?"

Burke didn't wait to be walked to the door. She was happy just to get away from the overgrown jerk. Once outside, she took a deep breath of the cool, crisp mountain air. "I think Nathaniel's wrong. Gambling isn't that jerk's problem. It doesn't matter how much talent he has. I guarantee that guy has a hard time keeping customers."

Stanley opened the driver's side door. "Perhaps you're right. No matter to us, though. What we do need is a better source of information. This one was, as they say, a total bust."

Burke pulled her phone out from her back pocket to look up the next address on the list Nathanial had given the and saw she had a message from Gordon—the man she'd met on their cruise.

When you get a chance, let me know you're okay.

She typed a message and sent it off.

I'm fine. Call you later.

Then she opened the map on her phone and found Kathy Montoya, a Wiccan who worked at a bookshop in Las Dos. She told the men and added, "And there's Sister Mary Catherine in Cañada de Los Alamos."

Stanley pointed the shapely nose of the Cadillac southeast.

CHAPTER THREE

Greg

GREG LAY ON HIS SIDE WITH HIS HAND IN THE CURVE OF ANNIE Kay's waist, just where it swelled upward toward her lovely round hip. The struggle between the desire to let her sleep and the urge to wake her up was real. He longed to make love to her. No woman had ever responded to him the way Annie Kay did. He'd known a lot of women, and a good many of them took a great deal of pleasure in sex, but none of them gave themselves over to it like Annie Kay. At the same time, watching her sleep filled him with a quiet satisfaction he wasn't sure he'd ever experienced before.

When he was married to Burke, they'd watched some chick flick where the male character declared, *"You complete me."* Greg laughed and Burke had gotten annoyed.

Now he understood.

Annie Kaye completed him. No longer did he need to roam around searching for meaning.

She sighed in her sleep and turned to nestle against his chest.

He wrapped his arms around her, breathed in the scent of her hair, and thought about the miraculous way she came into his life.

He'd been living with the witch in Colorado. Of course, he didn't understand at the time that she was actually a witch. He thought it was some sort of hobby, maybe a fashion statement or a metaphor. In his mind, witches were girls who wore a lot of black, and dyed their hair unnatural shades, and had an odd affinity for candles. By the time he figured out that the psycho actually thought she could cast spells and summon spirits, he was in hot water up to his neck. Things started to get ugly, so he took her spell book and ran.

In retrospect, he couldn't even say why he'd taken the book. He'd been angry. He knew she cared about that stupid book more than she cared about any living person. He wanted to make her mad. It seemed like a good idea at the time.

He'd had his doubts at first. Guilt had pricked at his mind as he drove past the Denver city limits with the book on the car seat beside him. He wasn't a thief and hurting her just for the sake of hurting her was petty. He was man enough to admit that, but now that he had the book, there was something about it.... He didn't want to let it go.

The first night, he checked into a Hyatt Place in Colorado Springs. He carried the book into his room, and while he ate Chinese carryout, he flipped through the pages, and tried to sound out the Latin words. He even looked a few of them up on Google Translate.

The little bit of the subject matter that he could grasp seemed dark to say the least—it was all stuff about death and darkness and decay. Nevertheless, the book felt special. Running his hands over the pages gave him a strange sense of power that he found rather enjoyable.

What wasn't enjoyable was the next day when he began to get the sense that someone was following him. For the first time, he truly feared that the witch had some kind of real power and she'd done something—hexed him, put a curse on him, sent some dark force to find and punish him for leaving her.

Women had a hard time getting over him.

But everything changed in Santa Fe. He searched for answers and, while not one of the people he'd spoken to offered any useful information, the book itself answered his plea and offered him a companion.

He found the book lying open and translated the first line on the page.

To be performed in a place of burial.

Certain he'd left the tome closed, convinced against all reason that the book itself was leading him, he decided to take the plunge. If the witch was using dark magic against him, the best answer was to protect himself using dark magic. At least, it was a better answer than any he'd gotten from the hippies and beatniks he'd spoken with the past several days.

He drove to Rosario Cemetery. The place bore little resemblance to the burial places he was familiar with in Michigan where lush green grass and towering maple trees grew between the long rows of gravestones. Here, headstones were propped up amid a sea of small round rocks. In some places, bricks outlined the rectangular perimeter of a grave. To Greg, it felt harsh and barren, but it was a place of burial and that's what he needed.

He carried the book under his arm to a sheltered spot under a mesquite tree and sat down beneath the gnarled branches with his legs crossed like a child. Reading the Latin text was tricky. A quick glance around assured him he was alone. No one would be around to laugh at him if he sounded ridiculous as he sounded out the unfamiliar words.

Spellwork turned out to be significantly more difficult than simply reading the words. Some part of himself, the same part that wanted more desperately every day to keep the book close at hand, poured energy into the words and phrases. Despite the chilly temperature, sweat dribbled down his temples and threat ened to drop in his eyes, but he couldn't have stopped for anything. Even if he could have, he wouldn't have. It was like the moment just before climax.

He began to chant.

Tionem animi invocabo.

Audite me. Surgere. Vocatus responderit.

Parere me. Surge. Venit ad dominum tuum.

The book began to grow warm in his hands.

Venit tempus.

Excitaret.

Resurgemus.

A ghostly shape floated up from a nearby grave, a woman in a Victorian dress. She turned toward him and stared with translucent eyes. A strange odor that brought to mind the stink of sulfur and the aroma of roses mixed together in a strange brew filled his mind and made him as dizzy as if he were sniffing glue.

I can't stop now. I'm so close.

Close to what, he couldn't exactly say. He'd know when he arrived at his destination. He turned the page and read on, sounding out each syllable with careful intention.

The spirit of the woman took on flesh. Light and shadows played off her form and her eyes widened. She held her hands out in front of her and stared at them. Seeing her standing there, a real woman of flesh and blood, and a gorgeous one at that, broke his concentration. He gaped at what he'd done.

Her form flickered and smoke rose from her clothing. "Don't stop," she pleaded. "It's not finished."

Blistering heat seared his hands, but he knew he had to finish. He screamed the last two lines of the spell, then dropped the smoking tome.

The girl blinked wide green eyes and smiled. "You did it."

He rose on legs as stiff as wood. Pins and needles pricked his feet, asleep from sitting on the ground as he had, and he stumbled toward her.

Her words came in breathless gasps. "You raised me from Perdition."

Thoughts ran through his mind, sluggish as mud sliding down a hill. A single idea rose above the others and consumed him. "We're not safe. We need to leave here." He gathered the book and held it close to his heart. The girl's hand slipped into his and he looked into her shining eyes. "I'll take care of you."

When she smiled, little dimples appeared in her round cheeks. "And I, you."

He half stumbled to the car, pulling her along. She took a moment to study the vehicle, then slipped into the front passenger seat without a word. He hurried around the hood and got into the driver's seat, then put the book on the back seat.

"We're going to go fast," he told her.

She held tight to the door with her right hand and the center console with her left and nodded, only uttering a single soft gasp when he pulled onto the road and accelerated to thirty-five miles per hour. Greg glanced at her from the corner of his eye, as if to assure himself she was really there, then looked forward again.

I raised a woman from the dead. A woman who, I'm guessing, has been dead for quite a while. What does that mean? What do I do with her now? Where do we go?

One certainty rolled through his mind, knocking the other thoughts aside like so many bowling pins.

The witch will kill me for this.

He swallowed the lump in his throat and turned into the hotel parking lot.

The girl leaned forward and gazed up at the five-story building. "You live here?"

"It's just a hotel."

"It's beautiful," she whispered.

Was it? With its fake stucco walls and uniformly placed windows it looked like pretty much every other hotel in a five hundred mile radius.

They exited the car and he led her up the sidewalk to the main entrance. She gasped when the glass doors slid open upon their approach, and she gaped at the marble front desk behind which stood a young man in a navy blue suit who looked consumed with boredom, no matter that a woman in a hundred-year-old gown was passing through the lobby. They entered the elevator and she clutched Greg's hand when the elevator jolted upward. She then spent the first five minutes in the room wandering from item to item, running her fingertips over everything.

"What year is it?" she finally asked. He told her and she rewarded him with her deep dimples. "My name is Annie Kay Morrison."

"I'm Greg Martin."

"You are a powerful necromancer."

He realized he'd been standing in front of the closed door, holding the book and staring at her like some sort of idiot. He set the book on top of the dresser.

"I'm just Greg."

Everything sort of happened in a blur then. She said something about how much she'd been missing life, and he said something about wishing for a companion. She went into the bathroom and the next thing he knew, she emerged in pure naked glory, her perfect curves fully exposed and utterly defiant of gravity.

His voice cracked like he was fifteen years old again. "Annie Kay?"

"That's me, and you're The Necromancer."

Uncomfortable laughter popped out of his mouth before he could stop the reaction. "I'm just Greg," he said again.

Good God, were her breasts that gorgeous in her first life or was that a perk of being undead? *Ha. Perk.* Blood rushed to his cheeks, and other locations as well.

She fluttered her long lashes. "You're very powerful."

He swallowed the lump in his throat. "Nah, just a guy."

When she took a step toward him, everything jiggled fantastically.

"You're so much more than just a guy." She stepped closer and pressed her hand over his heart. "You're so warm, so *alive*."

Taking on a mind of their own, his hands slipped around her slim waist. "You too," he managed.

"Thanks to you." She came even closer now, pressing those lovely breasts right up against him. "I'm so grateful. You have no idea what you took me from. You saved me."

"Glad I could help."

"I want you to know, Greg."

The heat of her body burned through his clothes to his flesh. "Know what?" His voice squeaked at the end of the short question.

"Know how grateful I am, of course, and how loyal I am. I'm yours now, Greg. In every way. Yours to command." She wrapped her arms around his neck. "Tell me what you want."

He'd been with a lot of women. Maybe too many. He was man enough to admit his weakness. He loved to be in love. He loved the way a woman's soft curves molded to his body. He loved the little gasping noises they made when they got excited. He loved the way they smelled, and the way they tasted, and the way they looked. But of all the women he'd ever known, he couldn't think of a single time one had pressed her naked body up against him and asked what he wanted. Now that the moment had come, he couldn't have spoken if his life depended on it.

She giggled. "Don't worry about it, lover. I feel what you want."

She undulated her hips against him, and he groaned and prayed he wouldn't embarrass himself. Next thing he knew, he stood before her as naked as she was and, sure enough, she made those little gasping sounds and as well as many others.

After, they lay on the mattress and she curled into the crook of his arm. "I'm safe with you, right?"

He kissed her lovely dark hair. "Of course."

"You won't send me back?"

"Never," he promised.

"Will you protect me?"

He squeezed her tighter. "Against every big, bad boogeyman who comes along."

"You know I depend on you, right? You understand that? The very breath in my body is drawn from an account that you control."

Her words stirred a frenzy in him again, and she proved to him that she really was willing to show her gratitude in all sorts of delightful ways.

He'd been waiting his whole life to meet a woman like Annie Kay. Who knew so much good would come from the witch's hurtful betrayal? Clearly, she'd never understood who he was at all, but this woman knew him already. This woman was meant for him.

CHAPTER FOUR

Richard

THEY DECIDED TO STOP AT THE BOOKSHOP IN LAS DOS BEFORE going on to Cañada de los Alamos. Back when Barbara was still alive, she used to love dragging Richard into stuffy little shops with too much brick-a-brack on the shelves. None of it was useful, and most of it was fragile, and he'd trail around behind her, hands in his pockets as his mother had taught him when he was a little boy, feeling like bull in a china shop. After she passed, he never felt a need to enter a single one of those places again.

Now here he was, hands in his pockets, standing between Burke and Stanley, trying not to knock over a shelf full of little glass statues with holes in them. They weren't even pretty. Looked like the plumbing under a bathroom sink, and the whole place stunk like a skunk infestation. Richard wrinkled his nose against the smell and wondered if he ought to say something about hiring a fumigator. Maybe the owner had something wrong with her sense of smell and she hadn't noticed the reek. It could be driving off customers and she wouldn't even know. Mentioning the stench would be doing her a favor.

Burke was explaining how they'd misplaced her ex-husband and someone mentioned he might have been in the shop at some point in the not-so-distant past. The Wiccan sucked on a lollipop while she listened. She was a plump woman, older than Burke and younger than Richard with an astonishing crown of flame-red hair.

When Burke finished her spiel, the woman grinned at Stanley. She pulled the sucker from her mouth with a pop. "What's you're roll in all this, Big Daddy?"

Stanley stood with his hands folded primly in front of him. "The three of us work together in most cases."

"You like threesomes?" She cackled at her own sick joke. "I saw your boy." She jammed the sucker back into her mouth. The sound of the candy clacking around her back teeth made all the little hairs on Richard's arms stand on end. "He came in here asking about protection from a witch."

"What did you tell him?" Burke asked.

"I told him to burn sage and stop whoring around. He seemed to take offense at the implication, but I've been on this earth long enough to spot a man who can't keep control of his magic wand. If you know what I mean."

Richard wandered away, pretending to be interested in a display of colorful rocks. Why the heck was everybody always talking about Greg's junk? What was the world coming to?

"Did he take your advice?" Stanley asked.

"He said it seemed stupid to pay good money for sage when the stuff grew wild on every roadside around here."

"Were you offended?" Burke asked.

"Oh, honey. It takes a lot more than that to break through this tough old hide," she said past the sucker.

Richard circled around the shelf and came back to the front to find Stanley pawing absently through a pile of little black prayer cards. "I'm surprised you remember him," Stanley said. "A man looking for protection from a former lover must not be so unusual for you."

She propped her forearms on the sales counter, giving Stanley and everybody else with a pair of eyes a view of her wrinkled old bosom. "I got a mind like a steel trap, lover. I got other things like a steel trap, too, if you care to investigate further."

Richard harrumphed. Crazy old bat. Did she honestly believe the prospect of sticking his willy in a steel trap was sexy? Then he thought about Stanley and his bizarre relationship with The Devil and things inside his head took a distinctly unpleasant turn. He stepped back and bumped into the shelf of weird glass tubes, nearly knocking it over. Burke shot him an evil look. He shrugged. Accidents happened. Maybe the old loon ought to make her aisles wide enough to accommodate a regular sized human being. Maybe she ought to get rid of all this crap and stock more than three shelves worth of books if she was going to bill her business as a bookstore.

"Do you have any idea where he might have been going? Did he leave any clue about how we might find him?" Burke asked.

"He said he was headed to the commune out by Clines Corners, I told him straight out that place wouldn't be a good fit for him. They live clean and simple, and they expect each member to pull their fair share. Your boy wouldn't make it a day, I'd wager. Too prim. He's a city-dweller in love with his vices. Whether he took my advice or not, I couldn't tell you. He was nervous though. I don't know if the evil chasing that boy was real or in his head, but it was real to him. That was plain as the nose on his pretty-boy face."

Burke handed her a business card with vague identification and real phone numbers. "Thank you for your time. If you think of anything at all that you feel might be helpful, please don't hesitate to give us a call."

The woman stood upright and cocked one hip forward. "Gladly." She winked at Stanley. "See you later, lover."

Stanley bowed like it was 1874 and the woman was part of the queen's court.

Richard stamped back out to the parking lot, wondering how long they'd end up chasing their tails before they came up with anything useful.

"Dick, down!" Stanley shouted behind him.

Richard dropped to the pavement so hard the wind got knocked straight out of him. The next thing he knew, Burke fell next to him and rolled until she banged into the side of the car.

She turned her head and he saw a trickle of blood running from a cut on her cheekbone. "Ghosts," she said.

Richard rolled onto his back to find two filmy white forms with red eyes bearing down on them. The squeaky hinges of the car's trunk screeched and, in the next moment, the unmistakable hard click of a shotgun being pumped sounded and the weapon roared twice in quick succession. Rock salt sprayed into the air and the forms burst into clouds of light that melted away like snowflakes. Burke pushed herself to her hands and knees and got to her feet.

Stanley came around the car and extended a hand to Richard. "Pretty quick reflexes, Dick. Well done."

"Better than me," Burke said. "I never saw the stupid thing coming."

Richard ignored Stanley's hand and wrestled gravity until he was in a more-or-less upright position again. His bad hip scolded him, but he diligently ignored it.

"Where'd they even come from?" he demanded.

Stanley tossed the shotgun back into the trunk. "I have no idea, but something tells me they're connected to everything that's been going on."

"Why would ghosts be connected to Greg?" Burke asked. "Unless.... You don't think he's one of them?"

"One of those?" Stanley gestured toward the spot the spirits had been before he shot them. "No. Those were old spirits, practically formless."

"Then how are they connected?" she asked.

"I don't know. Maybe they're not. It's just a hunch." Stanley tapped a forefinger against his chin. "Then again, perhaps Greg's disappearance led us to Santa Fe for a hunt that doesn't directly involve him."

Richard reached for the front passenger door handle. "Either way, I vote we get out of here before those things come back. Salt will scatter them, but that don't mean they're gone for good."

CHAPTER FIVE

Burke

THE COMMUNE THE OLD GAL IN THE BRICK-A-BRACK STRORE had spoken about wasn't actually in the little village of Clines Corners, but nearby under the shelter of a half-circle of ancient stones carved by the wind to resemble a Titan child's building blocks. Tiny hand-built adobe homes leaned at strange angles, and clear gaps showed between the tops of the walls and the corrugated tin roofs. Two women sat in aluminum lawn chairs, peeling the skins from a tub full of potatoes and tossing the skins to some scrawny chickens pecking in the snow nearby. A pair of demin-clad legs stuck out from under a pick-up truck that had been new when Burke was learning her ABCs.

"Greg wouldn't have lasted a day here," Burke said.

Richard twisted in the front passenger seat with a grunt to face her. "The smelly witch said they had a lot of rules."

Burke shook her head. "It's not about the rules. I mean, she's not wrong that he wouldn't do well with all that, but Greg loves luxury. These people live far too simply for his tastes."

They rolled past a goat in a little wire pen. The animal stared at them with bland curiosity.

"Not sure simple's the word I'd pick," Richard mumbled.

Stanley brought the Cadillac to a halt, then shifted into park. They all climbed out into a cold wind. The hands of the women never stopped their work, but their attention shifted onto the new arrivals.

"Good morning," Stanley called out as he approached them.

The woman on the left nodded, sending her mess of curls bobbing gently. The one on the right continued to stare.

"We were wondering if you could help us," Stanley said.

The curly-haired woman tossed her peeled potato in a pot of water and wiped her hands on an apron made out of a man's shirt. "Are you lost?"

Her voice took Burke off guard, soft as a young girl's with a slight French accent.

Stanley tucked his hands in his pockets and rocked on his toes. "No, ma'am, but I confess to taking a few wrong turns on the way to find this place. It's lovely, but a bit off the beaten path."

"That's the point," the other woman said in the gravely tones of a heavy smoker.

Burke pulled up the picture of Greg on her phone and walked over to the women. "We're trying to find my ex-husband. Have you seen him?"

"Why are you trying to find him?" the smoker asked.

"We have reason to believe he's in trouble," Burke said.

The woman scoffed. "For not paying child support or some such nonsense?"

Burke wondered what kind of woman thought child support was nonsense, but she left it alone and stuck to the topic at hand. "We believe he was running from someone who might have been trying to harm him, and then he disappeared. We don't know what happened, but we want to make sure he's safe."

The French woman started on another potato. "If he broke your heart, why do you care?"

Why did everyone keep asking her that? Wasn't it possible to be divorced from a man without wanting him dead? Of course, she *had* wanted him dead for a while. Kind of. During the same time she desperately wished he'd come back to her. Love was weird.

The man who'd been under the car meandered in their direction. Grease covered his hands, his overalls, and a good portion of his sun-weathered face. A gray stocking cap was pulled down over longish red curls.

"You looking for the guy with the face and hair?" he asked.

Richard opened his mouth and Burke hurried to speak before he did. "I'm not sure what you mean."

The man scoffed. "You know. He didn't look like normal folk. He looked like he belonged on television." His eyes traveled the length of her. "You do, too, for that matter."

Burke showed him the picture and he chuckled. "Yeah, that's him. You divorced a guy that looked like that? He must be a real jerk."

Must *everyone* have an opinion?

"So, he was here?" she asked.

"Yup. For about a minute. Sputtered something about wanting to live clean, then he just kinda wandered back to his car and high-tailed it out of here."

The smoker laughed, coughed, wheezed, and spit into the dirt. "He didn't wander. He saw Maude carrying chamber pots to the latrine pit and ran so fast he nearly tripped over his own feet."

Richard chuckled. The woman's mirth died into a glare that she turned on him as if his laughter were a deep offense.

"Any idea where he may have gone?" Stanley asked.

"None at all," the man said. "But I'd be willing to bet they've got flushing toilets wherever he ended up."

Burke thanked them all for their time and turned to go back

to the car, inwardly groaning at the idea of returning so soon to the confines of the Cadillac. It hadn't been the longest drive they'd ever taken, but it ranked right up there among the bumpiest, and she wasn't sure her backside was recovered enough yet to deal with the next round.

"Can I ask you something?" Stanley was still rooted to his spot, head cocked to one side. Burke halted and waited to see what he was going to say.

"Go on, then," the other man said.

"Have you noticed anything unusual lately?"

The women exchanged a long glance before turning their attention to the man.

"Not sure what you mean," he said.

Stanley lifted his shoulders slightly. "Anything at all—a weird smell in the air, maybe? Or everyone woke up from a nightmare on the same night? Or maybe chilly spots where it should be warm."

The man shook his head. "We live in houses that let the snow in if the wind is blowing hard. Chilly spots are nothing unusual, and like you heard, we use chamber pots, so we're accustomed to many smells. I guess we're not much help to you."

Stanley tangled his head. "I thank you for your time."

"There was a morning—about a week ago." The woman with the accent spoke up. "All the babies started crying at once. Even the older kids. Like something jumped up and scared them, but not one of them could tell us what the fuss was about." She stood and stretched her back. "We gave them apples and milk, and they were back to their games in no time."

Burke let Stanley give their thanks and goodbyes while she climbed back into the car, dreading the bumps but grateful to be out of the chilly wind. She couldn't quite imagine sitting outdoors in these temperatures while handling wet produce.

To each their own, I guess.

The men clambered into the front seat.

"Where to next?" Richard asked.

"If we stick to the plan, we head into town now," Burke told him. "Nathanial said from the beginning that this guy, Kenneth was our best bet. We could just—"

"No," Richard said. He yanked his seat belt across his chest and rammed it into the catch. "I ain't going to a haunted old folk's home."

Burke leaned over the back of the seat. "Grandpa, maybe we could just—"

"No."

"We could probably—"

"No."

Stanley started the engine and turned the car around. "Don't give it a moment's thought, Dick. Our trip into Santa Fe won't be wasted. We have it on good authority that our boy spent three days at the spa there. Surely, in three days' time he said something important to someone."

Richard drew back from Stanley. "The naked place?"

Stanley grinned. "There are documented health benefits to spending time in one's natural state, Dick."

Burke scooted back into her seat and pondered what life would have been like if she'd stayed on the cruise ship with Gordon, instead of coming in search of her ex-husband.

CHAPTER SIX

Greg

ANNIE KAY'S WONDERMENT OVER EVERY DETAIL OF THE WORLD delighted Greg. She walked through the local Wal-Mart with the wide-eyed reverence of a pilgrim at Mecca. The hotel swimming pool elicited squeals of joy. He worried that she'd faint when he used the hotel phone to call for pizza. It made him wonder what she'd think of the iPhone he'd tossed out the window back in Colorado when he first started getting the feeling he was being tracked.

She exhausted him with questions. The news, the television itself, the food they ate, the workings of the car—everything elicited another dozen queries. Finally, as they dined in their hotel room, wrapped in sheets and sipping good beer, he put a finger over her lips.

"My turn. I have questions too, you know."

Annie Kay kissed the finger pressed against her lips. "What would you like to know, my lord?"

He could get used to being called my lord. "Well, when everything first happened, when you first came to me, I was trying to wrap my mind around…you. The way you came to me. What I did to bring you here."

She nibbled a french fry.

Lucky french fry.

"I'm not sure I'll ever fully wrap my mind around all this," he said. "I mean, you came back from the dead. That's not a thing that happens."

"I suspect it happens more often than you realize," she said with no trace of sarcasm.

"So, what? The zombie apocalypse already happened, and no one noticed?"

"What is a zombie?" she asked.

He wrapped one of her soft curls around his finger. "You're a zombie, Annie Kay."

"Oh, well, then no. I'm unique. What you did, not many would do."

Greg shifted and set his half-full bottle of beer on the bedside table. "Okay, you've said something like that a few times and I've thought about it, and I have to ask why not? I mean, someone dies, you miss them terribly. If the magic exists to bring them back just as whole and lovely as ever, why not use that magic? Word would get out."

Annie Kay's eyes twinkled in the soft glow of the lamp. "You're too modest. Most sorcerers lack your immense courage."

"I appreciate your faith in me, Babe, and I don't want to burst your bubble or anything, but all I did was read some words from a book. It's not like I faced armies."

"Well, no, not *yet,*" she said.

Greg scratched the scruff on his chin. Time to shave. He hated the feeling of hair on his face. He often shaved twice a day, but he'd been distracted by this girl who wanted so badly to grant his every wish as if she were some sort of lovely, naked djinn.

"I won't face armies *ever,* Doll. I'm a lover, not a fighter."

She pushed into a kneeling position facing him on the bed.

"You raised me from Perdition. Now you must raise others. Raise your army. You can rule as king. You could go to war against Heaven itself."

He pressed his palm against her cheek and marveled at the soft warmth of her skin. "Okay. We'll lay our plans about storming the gates of Heaven another time. For now, explain why you say there are others raised from the dead, but you're unique."

"It is one thing to raise a person from the dead. There are ghosts, roaming the earth, that long to return to the flesh. There are spirits in Heaven, watching over their loved ones, waiting for the call. You raised me from Perdition."

"Yes, so you keep saying. What does that even mean?"

She pushed the food out of the way and sat on his lap, nuzzling beneath his chin like a baby kitten. "I was in Hell, doomed to eternal torment. The Devil Herself took her pleasure in torturing me, and when she—"

"Wait." He pushed her away and studied her pretty up-tilted eyes for any sign of teasing. "The Devil is a woman?"

Annie Kay nodded. "She's beautiful, and terrible. She smells like roses and her joy can make a brave man vomit until he bleeds."

Greg snickered. "Sounds like my ex-wife."

"You laugh because you can't imagine, but you saved me from her. You tore me directly from her grasp." She snuggled against him again. "It amazes me that you could be so brave."

While it was nice to bask in her praise, he couldn't in good conscience let her blow things so far out of proportion. "Really, Annie Kay, I'm glad it worked out well for you, but all I did was read some words from a book. I didn't fight a mighty battle or anything of the sort."

"Not yet, of course. But when she comes for you, you will fight."

He pushed her away again. "Excuse me?"

"I know you will be magnificent," she said breathlessly.

"Magnificent?" Surely, he was misunderstanding. A lot of new things had come to light in recent days. Apparently, witchcraft was a real thing. Heaven and Hell were literal places. Ghosts walked the earth, and pretty girls from the Old West could be brought back to life. Still...fighting The Devil Herself? That strained credibility for even the most open-minded liberal thinker.

"When she comes, you will stand strong," Annie Kay said. "The Devil is death, but death holds no power for you."

He squeezed her plump bottom. "Your faith is adorable."

"My faith in you is unshakable. When The Devil comes—"

"Babe," he cut in, "if The Devil shows up outside of my hotel room, my plan is to high-tail it out of town faster than a—"

"No!"

Her shout startled him into silence.

"You can't leave this town," she said.

He frowned. "What? Why not?"

The idea of staying in this dusty old town repulsed him. It was all well and good for a visit, but he preferred lush green grass beneath his feet and modern skyscrapers on the horizon.

"I can't leave this place," she said. "I died here. My life-force is tied to this place. Don't leave me, Greg." She seized his shoulders and as her panic rose, her long, sharp nails dug deeper into his flesh. "Don't leave me. I'll die. She'll take me back. I can't go back. I'll do anything. I'll give you anything. Just don't go."

"Shhh." He pressed his fingers to her pretty lips. "Be still. I won't leave you. We'll figure it out, okay?"

A little line formed between her brows. "What are you not saying?"

He smiled. "I'm not sure what you mean."

"There's something on the tip of your tongue, but you reign it in. What are you hiding?"

He lifted his hands, palms out. "I'm an open book. I promise."

Truthfully, he couldn't stop thinking about the witch. He'd

suspected for some time that she'd been using some kind of magic to follow him. Now, that power seemed to be broken, as if by using magic, he'd broken her power over him. But clever searchers found determined hiders all the time with no more than wits and shrewd guesses. Being shielded from magic wouldn't protect him from a good detective.

"You won't leave town?" Annie Kay asked.

"I promise," he said again.

After all, he had no plans to leave town that day. Let the next day worry about itself.

CHAPTER SEVEN

Burke

BURKE ASSUMED THAT THERE MUST BE SOME REASON THAT A particular geographical area was set apart and given a name, but she couldn't figure out what that reason was in the case of Cañada de los Alamos. They'd caved into Richard's insistence and skipped going to Santa Fe for the time being. While they drove, she didn't see a thing that indicated a village of any sort. The only signs of life were a few green road signs counting down the miles to the city limit. Then Stanley turned off the highway onto a road that someone had paved at some point in long ago history. After another three or four miles, he hung a left onto snow covered dirt that was smoother than the crumbling asphalt. Three or four miles after that, the dirt degenerated into little more than twin tracks through thick, scratchy flora that stuck up out of the sparkling blanket of snow.

The high desert wasn't friendly to fine automobiles. No way any of their recent travels were good for the Caddy's paint job. Stanley would be making friends with some local body shop owner in no time. Burke mused that if they ever had to search for

Stan the way they were searching for Greg, the local car guys might remember him just as well as the local hunters.

They came across an ancient, rusted motorhome that appeared to have half-melted into the earth from which it had come. It sat in a depression that looked like it had been carved out of the earth by a meteor. Smoke rose from a homemade chimney pipe and curled toward skyward as if hoping to become clouds.

Three SUVs, a small school bus sans tires, a Smart Car, and a 1976 Mercury Cougar were parked in a haphazard fashion at the end of the trail. Stanley added the Cadillac to the collection, and they piled out. Richard hoisted himself up with some difficulty using the door and the back of the seat.

"You okay?" Burke asked as she pulled the zipper up on her puffy pink coat and checked that the pocket holding her gun was unsnapped. "Fine as frog's hair," he muttered. "This cold weather don't help my hip."

"That fall couldn't have been very good either." She wished he would sit this one out in the car.

"Yeah, well, I'm still able to sit up and take nourishment. I reckon I'll live," he said, as if reading her mind.

Discomfort was written in each of his steps, but Burke knew better than to fuss at him about it. Stanley knocked on the flimsy door. While they waited for an answer, a gentle flurry began to fall, though Burke couldn't tell from where. The wispy white clouds overhead didn't seem capable of producing any real precipitation.

With a squeak that sounded like a cat that had been stepped on, the door opened, and a woman stood before them, tiny, ancient, and wrinkled as a raisin with a pure white braid that hung to her knees. She peered at them over the rims of half-moon spectacles that had one arm held together with electrician's tape.

"Mrs. Perez?" Stanley asked.

If staring were an Olympic sport, this woman would have a

rack of gold medals. Her unblinking gaze honed in on Stanley and she gave a single nod.

"My name is Stanley Kapcheck," he said. "These are my associates, Richard and Burke. We were wondering if we could ask you a few questions."

Elvira Perez, the sixth person on Nathanial's list of seven, leaned forward so far Burke worried she might topple through the narrow doorway. She sniffed the air around Stanley and frowned.

"May we come in for a moment?" Stanley asked.

"No."

Burke slipped her hands into the pockets of her coat and felt the weight of her gun there. She didn't know why this little old lady caused the hairs on the back of her neck to stand on end, but if she'd learned anything in the last year it was to trust her gut. Something was off here.

Stanley inclined his head. "I understand. Perhaps you could tell us if you know this man." He held his phone up for the woman to see, but her gaze didn't leave his face.

"What have you done?" she asked.

"Excuse me?" Stanley asked.

"You stink of the white devil."

Composed as ever, Stanley moved the phone a little closer to her. "Greg is Burke's ex-husband. We have reason to believe he's in trouble and we're trying to find him so we can help."

"Are you a hunter?" she demanded.

Richard shuffled a step closer to Burke.

"Yes," Stanley admitted.

"Is he a monster?" She nodded toward the phone.

"No, but we're worried monsters may be pursuing him."

Fear flicked its forked tongue against the back of Burke's neck. Powdery snowflakes fluttered down to paint the red-rock landscape white. Far overhead, a bird of prey drew wide circles in the air. A chilly breeze carried the scent of juniper and sage. She scanned the surrounding area but saw nothing out of the ordinary.

So what? What am I missing?

Elvira stared at Stanley without blinking. "The Necromancer will open the gates and you will be forced to choose a side."

Stanley cleared his throat. "I appreciate the warning, ma'am, but we're wondering if you've seen Greg?"

Burke held her breath. *She hasn't blinked since she opened the door.* Burke studied the scrawny woman's sunken chest. No hint of a breath stirred the fabric of her faded housecoat.

"The Necromancer has been born. The dead will have dominion."

Burke tugged on the back of Stanley's jacket. "We should go, Stanley. Mrs. Perez obviously doesn't feel like talking to us."

The old lady's unsettling gaze shifted to Burke.

Richard brandished his pistol. "Regna terrae, cantata Deo, psallite--"

The old woman threw her head back and cackled. "I am not a demon, foolish old man."

Richard lowered his gun an inch or two. "I ain't that old."

"What are you?" Burke demanded of her. She drew her gun from her pocket and used it to cover her grandfather.

"I'm Elvira Perez."

Stanley rubbed his chin. "My friends sense something amiss. Perhaps we've misunderstood. Are you in trouble, my dear?"

Mirth shook her narrow shoulders. "Not anymore. My troubles have all come to an end, as they say." Her unblinking eyes studied each of them in turn. "Or they had, until hunters showed up at my door."

Low rumbling reached their ears and Burke turned toward the noise. A battered pickup missing its exhaust system barreled over the sorry excuse of a road and skidded to a stop not far from the Cadillac in a cloud of dust and snow. A small man with short-cropped hair leaped out of the driver's door.

"Don't hurt her!" he shouted.

Richard turned to face the newcomer. Stanley remained locked in a staring contest with the old lady.

"Don't hurt her," the man said again. "Please. I'm begging you."

The old woman cackled. Her hand shot out toward Stanley's throat, and he dodged left, whipped a pair of silver handcuffs from his jacket pocket, and slapped them on the woman's wrists. Tendrils of smoke rose from the places where metal touched flesh and she screamed and hissed and fell to her knees.

"Stop, please." The man tried to push through them, but Burke stepped in front of him, still pointing her weapon.

"Tell us what's going on," she demanded.

Tears pooled in the man's eyes. "Are you cops?"

Elvira fell back into her house and lay on her side, screaming. "They're hunters, Eddie! Kill them! Kill them!"

Eddie's shoulders slumped. "Please let her go."

"Tell us what happened," Burke ordered.

"Saturday, real early, she woke up sick," he said in a defeated voice. "I mean, she's been sick for just about forever, but it was bad. She called me, and I came as quick as I could, but by the time I got here she was just about gone." His voice cracked and he swallowed hard. "I held her, and she just got quieter and quieter and then...." A single tear rolled from the inner corner of his eye and cut a damp track down the side of his nose. "She was gone. I knew it was coming, but I just couldn't believe it."

"It burns! Make them stop!" she screamed.

Elvira twitched against her bonds, but Burke had no fear she'd break them. She'd seen the warded cuffs hold creatures significantly more powerful than whatever this woman was.

"So, you brought her back?" Stanley asked.

Eddie's eyes widened. "No, it wasn't like that. My people, we don't do that kind of thing. It never ends well. We know that."

Burke lowered her weapon. "But, clearly, she's back."

He sniffed and wiped his face with the sleeve of his heavy brown coat. "I didn't do it. I didn't do anything. She was gone, and then she wasn't. I didn't bring her back to me. She just *came* back."

"The Necromancer will give us dominion," Elvira whimpered.

Richard crossed himself, a gesture Stanley had taught them carried more power than people assumed.

Stanley's shoulders drooped and a look of genuine pain crossed his face. "It never ends well, Eddie."

Eddie sniffed again. "She's my mom, man. What am I supposed to do?"

Sadness welled in Burke's heart as the pieces fell into place. Somehow, and God only knew how, this woman died, fully crossed over, and almost immediately came back. Things that came back were invariably dangerous—violent and bloodthirsty and unpredictable. Truer words were never spoken. It never ended well.

Burke took a steadying breath and stuffed her gun back into her pocket. "Let's go sit in the car and talk, Eddie. It's warmer there."

He looked at the motorhome door where only Elvira's twitching feet could be seen and, in the high-pitched voice of a boy much younger than he was, he asked, "Can I say goodbye?"

"You already said goodbye. You held her close and you showed her your love, and you said goodbye, and your mom moved on."

"But..." He gestured vaguely, then his hand fell limp at his side.

Burke steered him toward the Cadillac, and they climbed inside while Stanley and Richard went into Elvira's house and shut the door.

"It's not really her. Not anymore," Burke said.

Eddie stared out the window.

"Your mom is gone. What's here now—that thing—is going to hurt someone, and you know that."

Silence.

A single muffled gunshot sounded from inside the house. Elvira's son covered his face with both hands and sobbed.

CHAPTER EIGHT

Greg

ANNIE KAY TRACED THE MUSCLES ON GREG'S STOMACH WITH one long, polished fingernail. "You know, in my day, only hussies and foreigners painted their nails."

"Which were you?" he murmured in a sleepy voice.

She gave him a gentle pinch and he chuckled.

"Now a woman can do just about anything she pleases to her own body and be celebrated for it. I like this time," she said.

"My ex would say women are still oppressed."

Annie's hand moved lower beneath the blanket. "It's all relative, I guess." She kissed his broad chest and caught his nipple between her teeth. "Men weren't so pretty then. I've never known anyone with more perfect teeth than you."

He pulled her hip closer. Fully awake, now, he was ready for her. Greg thought that maybe for Annie Kay, he'd be ready no matter how old he was or how long they'd been together. With a smile, she sat up and slung one leg over his body and straddled him. He sucked air through his teeth.

"You're so beautiful," he said.

"You too," she answered. "Not only that, you're interesting."

He shifted suddenly, ripping a gasp from her.

"You think?" he asked.

She exhaled slowly before answering. "Oh, yes."

"You're not just saying that because...you know." In lieu of explaining with words, he thrust his hips hard enough to draw a gasp of pleasure from her.

"Because of what you do in bed?" Annie Kay laughed.

He loved the sound of her joy. Other girls tittered and giggled. Annie Kay's laughter bubbled up like clear water from a mountain spring.

"Lots of men can do interesting things in bed," she said.

"You act interested when you're in bed." He slid his hands upward along her rib cage.

"You do well enough, sure. But there's so much more to you" she said in a breathless voice. "You drive fast. You drink the best whiskey. You dragged me out of Perdition."

He couldn't help but grin. "There's that."

"What else can you do?" she asked, moving faster.

He flipped her onto her back and pinned her wrists down on each side of her head. "What do you want me to do?"

"Raise an army of the damned. Lead them in a battle against Heaven. Sit me on the throne as your queen."

He buried his face in her neck so she wouldn't see the fear in his eyes. "Anything for you, Annie Kay. If that's what you want, I'll do it."

"God, I love being alive!" she cried.

WATER DRIPPED FROM GREG'S HAIR ONTO THE COLLAR OF HIS tee-shirt. Annie Kay had teased him about how often he showered, but she obviously liked it. She commented more than once that she'd never known a man who smelled so good, so often.

He'd never stopped to think of the body odor that must have hung like a cloud over every city before the days of indoor plumbing and deodorant.

"What should we have for dinner?" he asked. He plucked the credit card he'd lifted from some old geezer off the top of the hotel dresser and waved it in the air. "According to the name on this card, Mr. Brandon Henton is treating, and he says you can have anything you like." He figured there was no need to feel guilty about using Henton's card. The bank would reimburse him when he reported fraudulent charges anyway.

"Something fresh and green," she replied.

He slipped the card into his wallet and tucked the wallet in his back pocket. "More rabbit food?"

"You can eat lettuce and ripe tomatoes when there's snow on the ground." She grabbed her coat from the corner chair. "It's as much of a miracle as being rescued from Hell. I'll eat it every day."

He wrinkled his nose. "Fine. We'll find a steakhouse. You can eat garden weeds and I'll get a proper piece of meat. I don't want to stay out too long, though. This town—I can't shake the idea that there are eyes everywhere."

Her hand trembled as she fumbled with the zipper on her coat. "We can't leave here. You can't. You can't leave me."

Greg tugged the zipper up and pulled her into his arms. "I know. We'll figure it out, okay? But I don't want to put us in danger. That witch—" He broke off when she pulled away and looked into his eyes.

"Your fear of the witch baffles me." She actually sounded a little angry. "How can you fear a mere mortal who possesses a bit of magic when the entire underworld stands at your beck and call? She can't hurt you. You're so much bigger than anything around you. Even if she could, I wouldn't let her."

Even if he tried to convince her, she'd never believe he just stumbled through the spell that brought her back to life. What was the harm in letting her keep her illusions? Reasoning with himself was a perfected skill. *Isn't it better for her if she's not constantly living in fear?*

"You love me enough to protect me from the crazy women from my past?" he asked.

Annie Kay stretched on tiptoe and kissed his cheek. "Feed me dinner, then maybe I'll profess my love."

He chuckled and they went arm-in-arm from the little motel out into the big, bright, electrified whirlwind of the modern world.

Annie Kay squeezed his arm. "I don't think I felt this alive even when I was actually alive."

CHAPTER NINE

Richard

NONE OF THEM FELT MUCH LIKE TALKING, SO THEY MADE THE
trip from Cañada de los Alamos up to Chupadero in silence.
Father Patrick Park was the last name on the list Nathanial had
given them. A sense of calm settled over Richard when they
pulled up in front of the catholic church. The place seemed
neither ancient nor neglected. Adobe walls and a tin roof showed
just enough wear and tear that they no longer looked new, but not
so much one would assume the place had been collecting ghosts
for five hundred years. A wide walkway leading to the arched
wooden doors on the front of the building had been shoveled
clean and salted for safety. Richard felt confident that neither
restless spirits nor zombie Navajo women roamed the halls of
such a place.

Stanley tested the door, found it unlocked, and held it open
for Richard and Burke. A wooden stand held a bowl of holy water
in the narthex. Red carpet lined the aisle that led to the altar.
Votive candles flickered on low wooden tables near the front of
the church. A man who resembled a young Robert Redford in

blue jeans and a cleric's shirt tucked pencils into little holders on the backs of the pews. He looked up and flashed a movie star grin when they trooped through the door.

"Good afternoon," he said.

Stanley removed his hat. "Good afternoon. Are you Father Park?"

"I am." The priest lay his box of pencils on the nearest pew and met them halfway, extending a hand to Stanley.

When everyone had been introduced by first name, Burke showed him the photograph of Greg and gave the story about trying to find her ex-husband.

"Yes, of course. He stopped in only a few days ago," Father Park said without hesitation. "Last week, maybe? I suppose it must have been on a Wednesday because I was just getting ready to head downtown to the senior center to lead the weekly mid-week service there. He seemed troubled."

Burke tucked the phone back into the pocket of her jeans. "In what way?"

"Nervous, paranoid, even. He seemed to believe someone was using black magic against him."

"Were they succeeding?" Stanley asked.

Father Park studied Stanley for a long moment as if to determine whether or not he was being teased. "Do you believe in black magic, Mr. Kapcheck?"

"Oh, yes," Stanley said.

The priest blinked. Richard wondered what he'd expected Stan to say.

"Well, I told him to rest assured that no such thing could harm a blameless man," the priest replied.

Burke snorted. "Greg's not blameless."

"Is that why you're searching for him?"

"I just want to make sure he's okay," she said.

"I was just about to make a pot of tea. Would you all like to join me?" Father Park looked at each of them in turn.

Stanley accepted on their behalf, and the good-looking priest ushered them down a short hallway and into a commercial kitchen full of shiny stainless steel appliances. He gestured toward some tall stools and started fussing with a tea kettle. Stanley and Burke hopped up onto their seats with lithe grace. Richard held onto the counter for dear life and wiggled and grunted until his butt was planted on the chair.

"Do you have any idea where Greg might have been headed after talking with you?" Burke asked.

"I'm sorry, but he didn't say, so far as I can recall. I find it upsetting that he's disappeared, though. He seemed to be at his wit's end. He was getting desperate. That much was clear." The priest pulled four sturdy ceramic mugs from a cabinet near the stove and set them on the counter.

Stanley traced the handle of his cup with the tip of his forefinger. "There must be hundreds of churches in the Santa Fe area. I mean no offense by asking, but why do you think Greg might have singled this one out?"

The priest leaned against the counter and rested his hands on the edge. "Greg was concerned about black magic, witchcraft, evil spirits, that sort of thing. Some time ago it came to the attention of the local press that I've been trained by the Vatican to perform exorcisms. He told me he stumbled across the article during a visit to the library."

"Do you think demonic activity is involved in Greg's disappearance?" Burke's tapped her fingernails against the countertop in quick rhythm.

"Not so far as I could see." He threw the question back at her. "Do you think demonic activity is involved in Greg's disappearance?"

"At this point, I haven't the foggiest idea." She wrapped her hands around the empty mug, much to Richard's relief. The tapping nails sometimes seemed to be tapping right against his brain. "As far as I last knew, before this incident, Greg had no knowledge of, or belief in, anything supernatural," she went on. "He's not a religious man. He certainly wasn't one to fiddle with witchcraft. I can't imagine what he might have done to attract demonic attention."

The tea kettle whistled, and Father Park removed it from the burner and poured for all of them, then set a box of assorted tea bags on the counter. "Most people aren't so calm and open-minded about these topics. I'm assuming you all have some experience in dealing with these things."

Stanley plucked an Earl Grey from the box and unwrapped it. "You assume correctly, Father. I wonder, have you noticed anything strange in the past several days?"

"Oh, yes."

They all stared at him, waiting. Richard decided he'd had enough of chasing his tail around town learning a bunch of nothing and trying to be polite. As if ghosts and zombies weren't enough for one day, now they had to deal with some kind of second-rate sensationalist philosopher.

"You going to let the cat out of the bag or are we just going to sit here with our thumbs up our butts, playing twenty questions?" he demanded.

For his honest question, he was laughed at.

"Forgive me," the priest said. "I suppose I get in the habit of trying to draw people out and struggle sometimes to give straight answers." He sipped his tea with a noisy slurp. "Last Saturday I..." He hesitated.

"Well?" Richard demanded.

"Maybe I ought to show you." He led them back into the sanctuary and pointed to the statues along one wall of the church. All three hunters edged closer to them. At first, nothing appeared out of the ordinary, but upon closer inspection, dark tracks could be seen, dripping from the painted eyes.

"I tried to clean them, but the blood stained. So far no one has noticed, and I'm glad." The priest shook his head. "I don't know what I'd tell them."

Stanley touched the face of the Virgin. "They were weeping tears of blood?"

"They were. Every one of them."

Richard didn't even try to suppress the shiver that raced through him. "Saturday morning's the same time the old lady came back."

"What old lady?" Father Park asked. "Do you think this has to do with your missing man?"

Burke sighed and did to him what he'd done to her. "I don't know. Do you think it has to do with my missing ex-husband?"

Richard noticed she placed a heavy emphasis on the "ex."

The priest sat on the end of the nearest pew. "Who are you people, really?"

Stanley moved from statue to statue, checking out the creepy blood stains. "We're hunters," he said.

The priest clamped a hand over his mouth.

Richard harrumphed. "You perform exorcisms and you believe in black magic. You got statues crying tears of blood in your church, but three hunters show up and you get your drawers in a knot?"

The priest removed his hand from his mouth. "You're Stanley Kapcheck."

Finally, Stanley turned and met the man's gaze. "That's right."

"The demons...they...they speak of you."

Richard didn't know why this declaration should have surprised him. He'd found out pretty early on in their acquaintanceship that Stanley had literally been to Hell and back and he'd forged some sort of bizarre bond with The Devil Herself while he was there. Not so long ago, someone in a position to know had informed them that The Devil had issued a strict warning. None of the creatures under her command were allowed to harm

Stanley in any way. So far as Richard could figure, she was either planning to marry him or kill him herself. Could go either way.

Stanley smiled, but his eyes failed to do that scrunchy thing at the corners like they usually did. "Yes, well, I've been hunting a very long time."

"The Devil put her mark on you," Father Park murmured.

"Not quite," Stanley said. "Things haven't gone so far as all that."

"They've gone too far."

There was no arguing with that, Richard thought, and apparently Stanley agreed. He changed the subject back to the matter at hand. "I appreciate you taking the time to talk with us about Greg, Father. If you think of anything further, please do give us a call."

Burke handed him one of the little cards, and Father Park took it without looking at it.

"I don't know if you're the bravest or the most foolish people I've ever met," he said, still staring at Stanley.

Richard understood just where the guy was coming from. He didn't know, either.

CHAPTER TEN

Greg

G REG FIDDLED WITH THE BUTTER KNIFE, TWIRLING IT BETWEEN his fingers. Annie Kay had gone to use the ladies' room. Coming back to life meant dealing with all the human stuff. Nothing weird about using the bathroom.

At least, that's what he kept telling himself, but he couldn't quite convince himself it was true. Maybe if she'd just excused herself and danced through the busy restaurant in that direction, he wouldn't have thought too much about it. But she'd been off, ever since two guys got in a fight in the bar. Not much of a fight, really, as far as he'd seen from where he and Annie Kay sat. One guy yelled something about the other guy's wife. The second guy threw a punch. Blood splattered down the front of the first guy's shirt, and then the manager and a cook were hauling the two brawlers out the front door.

After the drama ended, Greg looked across the table to see Annie Kay white as a…well…as a ghost, to pardon the expression.

"Are you okay?" he'd asked.

"Fine, just a little startled."

But the ice in her water glass clinked in her shaking hand when she tried to take a sip, and conversation died down to single words and non-committal noises after that. She pushed the remainder of her salad around the plate with her fork, but never really took another bite, then she dropped her fork and ran off.

A stomachache, perhaps? Maybe the food was too rich?

Another ten minutes passed, and Greg gave into his nerves and asked one of the waitresses to check on her. But the place was a madhouse, and the girl never returned.

He drummed his fingers against the table, but that made him think of the way Burke always tapped her nails on everything, so he stopped. Twenty minutes. Something was definitely wrong. Maybe she really was sick. Maybe some psycho followed her into the bathroom. Maybe The Devil found her after all. Or the witch.

Greg wasn't sure which prospect frightened him more.

The vinyl seat bench squeaked under his weight when he shifted to stand, and his feet stuck to the floor as he wound his way around the crowded tables. Outside, a sign announced fine family dining, but apparently the owners had a loose definition of the word *fine*. In the long, narrow hallway that led to the bathroom, one of the fluorescent tubes flickered, giving a dizzying strobe effect.

He stopped outside the scarred swinging door marked, "gals" and cleared his throat. "Annie Kay?"

No answer, but he hadn't spoken very loudly and if there was water running or an electric hand dryer blasting hot air, it would be difficult to hear over. Pushing the door open only an inch or so, and careful to avert his eyes, lest anyone see him by the ladies' room and get the wrong impression, he called out again.

Was that tiny noise crying?

"Annie Kay, are you still in there? Are you sick, Babe?"

He glanced over his shoulder. No one paid him any attention. He faced the door and said, "I'm coming in unless someone tells me not to."

No one replied, but he was quite certain he heard weeping now. Exercising caution, in case he needed to beat a hasty retreat, he slipped through the door.

Red paint splattered everywhere—the wall, the mirror, the sink, and a great pool of it on the floor.

He grabbed the wall for support.

It has to be paint, still wet and glistening.

Then his gaze fell upon Annie Kay on the other side of a large plastic trash can, looking impossibly small with her knees drawn up to her chest and blood smeared across her face. Blood covered her hands and had soaked through the front of the new blouse she'd been so proud of.

He took a step toward her and caught sight of the waitress he'd asked to check on Annie Kay. She lay sprawled on the floor beside Annie Kay, her wide eyes staring blindly at the ceiling. Where her neck had been, was only mangled flesh.

The fear that held him motionless suddenly snapped into a different form and, in a flash, he was kneeling on the hard tile floor with his love in his arms as she sobbed against his chest.

"Tell me what happened," he said in a rush. "Are you hurt? Who did this?"

She pulled away from him and swiped at the tears on her face, leaving gruesome steaks of red. "I don't know what happened. I didn't mean to."

At the pace of a man trudging through knee-deep mud, Greg's mind began to connect the dots. There was blood on Annie Kay's mouth. The waitress's throat had been torn apart. He fought the urge to run to the nearest toilet and give up the meal he'd just eaten. Pins and needles pricked the tips of his fingers and toes. Bells rang in his ears.

He glanced around, though no one had entered. "We've got to get out of here."

Annie Kay nodded. Her wide eyes stared into his, but she didn't move.

Horror shot past panic and honed a sharp edge of a mental sword wielded by some cold, reptilian part of his brain that cared about nothing beyond survival.

"Get up, now." He kept his voice to a whisper. "Stop wasting time. We've got to go."

She let him lift her to her feet, and they stumbled across the few steps to the sink. He helped her scrub her hands and face while he tried not to think about what they would do if anyone decided to use the facilities. Once all but the worst of the blood was gone, Greg helped her into his coat and zipped it up. Unless someone looked very closely, they'd never notice the bits of dried blood around her fingernails or on her collar. Without another word, they slipped through the restaurant, heads down, out the front door, and into the car. If they could just get back to the hotel, that would buy them some time. Even if someone remembered them—and who would? They were just another couple eating nothing remarkable, doing nothing remarkable. He'd paid with someone else's credit card and....

The same credit card they'd used to pay for the hotel.

Panic threatened once again, but he gripped the steering wheel in tight fists and swallowed it down. Even if someone came for them, it would be hours before anyone pieced it all together and showed up at the hotel. He would take Annie Kay to the hotel, and she could clean up and change. He knew she couldn't leave town and if she couldn't, he couldn't, but it was a decent-sized city surrounded by rugged wilderness.

"We'll figure something out," he told her.

She nodded and offered him a trusting little smile, but he couldn't stop from wondering if that twinkle in her eye was adoration or something more closely resembling hunger?

CHAPTER ELEVEN

Burke

Burke suggested, and the men agreed, that they retreat to Nathanial's place. To say it had been a long day was the understatement of the century. Only two places remained on their list: the nudist spa and the haunted senior center. Despite the clear fact that they should have started at the senior center, no one was in a hurry to go now. Desperation to find Greg before something terrible happened—assuming nothing already had—gave way to an exhaustion of spirit. Exhaustion invariably brought slowed reflexes and muddied thinking. Wisdom counseled taking a break. They could head out fresh in the morning.

Nathanial fed them Navajo tacos on fat crispy-fried flour tortillas and listened intently to their retelling of the day's strange happenings while Jeremiah paced back and forth under the table and wove his sinuous body around the chair legs.

"I heard a lot of things from a lot of people, but not a thing that would help me say why all this is happening. Each incident on its own...." He shrugged. "Things like that can happen. But all together? I don't know what could cause that."

Burke gave voice to a terrible thought she'd had while they'd driven back to the cottage. "You don't think this has anything to do with The Children of Cain and the Daughters of Kali and all that, do you? They talked about opening portals between worlds."

Stanley closed the battered leather-bound journal he'd been paging through and pushed it aside. "Between worlds, yes, but this is different from that. This is more like the veil between life and death is failing."

"My money's on a witch," Richard said. He chugged the little glass of prune juice next to his plate. "The whole thing feels witchy to me."

Nathanial scooped Jeremiah up in one massive hand, cradled him against his chest, and started feeding him cheese shreds. "Maybe, but if it is, it's a powerful kind of witchcraft that no one in their right mind would fiddle with. If a witch powerful enough to cause these kinds of ripples through the region with her magic followed Burke's man, why hasn't she found and killed him, then gone on her way?"

Each question turned into a seed that grew a tree covered in the fruit of more questions. Burke excused herself to take a long run. When she returned, she pleaded exhaustion and went straight to her room. She loved all three men, but there were moments when she missed her quiet days of solitude.

OVER BREAKFAST, THEY DISCUSSED THEIR TWO REMAINING leads.

"Dick doesn't want to go to the retirement home, so that means we head to the spa," Stanley had said.

Burke shot him a look. Sometimes his teasing of Richard went just a bit further than was nice. On the other hand, sometimes it was very hard to tell when Stanley was teasing. No doubt the man would be as comfortable in a nudist spa as he would be in a

British tea room. Naked people weren't the kind of thing Stanley was likely to make a fuss about, and he had no shame in his own body.

"You want me to spend my day interviewing naked people?" Richard asked.

Hoping to intervene before her grandfather got worked into a lather, Burke leaned forward and put her hand over his. "We've got to do something. Yesterday was a bust. The clock is ticking. If you want to sit this one out—"

Richard barked back at her. "I ain't sitting on the sidelines." He sagged against the back of his chair. "I guess it only makes sense to go to the old folk's home, then. That's where the guy who talks to everyone works, right? Might as well get it over with."

After that, they all wandered off to their rooms to finish getting ready without much more discussion.

In her room, Burke tightened the laces on her boots and snugged a dagger into each boot's hidden sheath. The left dagger was sterling silver. The one on the right, iron. That one was so poorly made it barely held an edge sharp enough to slice butter, but it would take out any number of creatures from ghosts to fairies with a touch.

She rose and stretched, cracking her back. Her heart pumped hard and steady. For far too long, she had chased her self-esteem on a treadmill. She had reasoned that if her husband left her for an underwear model, the way to get him back was to be even more attractive that that twenty-something stick figure. When her grandfather pulled her into the crazy life of a hunter almost a year ago, she'd been thin and fit. But the kind of strength that comes from a gym and the kind that comes from battling creatures who can toss a grown man like a rag doll were not at all comparable. These days, she wasn't just fit, not just strong. She was powerful and she reveled in that knowledge.

She took her gun belt from the bedpost and wrapped it

around her waist, then picked up her phone and glanced at the screen to find Gordon had texted.

Did you find him?

She replied.

Not yet.

He responded immediately.

Worried?

Yes.

Should I be worried? he asked.

She stared at the message and chewed her lip. How to answer? In the great scheme of things, she'd only known Gordon for a hot minute. But that minute had been hot, indeed. When they parted ways—him to wrap things up on his job as the head of security on a cruise ship and her to rescue her idiot ex-husband—she'd been downright tingly at the thought of hunting with Gordon at her side.

And now?

A knock sounded at the door.

"It's me," her grandpa called.

"Come in."

Didn't she already have enough men around her? Did she really want one more? Not that having Gordon around was the same thing. Still....

Her grandpa opened the door and entered. "You look like your right-fielder's out peeing in the weeds."

She cocked her head. "What does that even mean?"

He blew a raspberry at her. "Stanley's warming up the Caddy."

"I'm ready to go," Burke told her grandfather, now that he was waiting for her, but first, she tapped the phone screen with her thumbs in reply to Gordon's message.

Worried about Greg and me? Not a chance.

A true statement. If she backed out of whatever it was that she and Gordon had together, it wouldn't be because of Greg.

Her grandfather waited by the door, fingers drumming against his thighs.

"What's with you?" she asked.

"What do you mean?"

"You're fidgeting. You're generally not a fidgety guy."

He stilled his hands by pressing his palms against his sides. "There."

Burke slipped her arms into the FBI jacket Stanley had provided without explanation as to where it had come from. She took a stab in the dark. "It must bring back some unpleasant memories, going to a nursing home."

"I'm fine." He fiddled with his hearing aid, sending a tiny squeak of feedback into the room.

"Well, I was thinking about it," Burke lied. She hadn't given her grandfather's protests much thought at all. She'd been too wrapped up in her own drama. "I think it's kind of cool, you know?"

Richard scowled.

"I mean, you were a total victim when mom put you in that place back home. Life had sort of steam-rolled you, what with the fall and getting hurt and everything, but then, right at the moment your number was called you sort of squared your shoulders and flipped the Grim Reaper the bird, and you've been doing it ever since. Now you get to spend whatever time you have left being the hero of your own story. You're amazing."

After several seconds, he swallowed hard. "All right then, let's go."

He squared his shoulders and led her through Nathanial's house toward the front door. She smiled at his back. She really was proud of him. A lot of people claimed to be too old to change. Richard had tried harder to better himself over the past year than anyone she'd ever known. He still had room for growth but, hey, didn't everyone?

The big guy stood in the kitchen wearing a grape-purple velour jogging suit and furry boots that came up to his knees. His bushy beard sported a new crop of little plastic beads.

"You all be careful," he said.

"You sure you won't come?" she asked.

Nathaniel twisted his hands. "Told you last time you passed through, I'm not a hunter. You come back here tonight, and we'll have dinner. I'll make turkey posole." He fished in a pocket and came up with a cord necklace bearing a small wooden ankh. "Wear this, will you?"

She took the necklace from him and ran her thumb over the symbol. It carried a patina that could only have been achieved by age.

"The ankh is a powerful symbol of life. That one's been blessed," he explained.

She slipped the cord over her neck and tucked the charm inside the front of her shirt. When someone like Nathanial handed you a charm, you'd be a fool to reject it.

"Thanks for everything, Nathanial. See you soon."

"I hope that's true," he said.

They found Stanley waiting in the driver's seat of the Cadillac. Richard took the passenger seat and Burke slid into the back. The V8 engine growled and the tires chewed through the skin of snow covering the road. Burke would have sworn that even the car was ready for this hunt. They'd had a rough stretch since Thanksgiving, but they were back to full power now that Stanley was himself again, and she pitied the creature that crossed their path.

Villa Cierto Retirement Home sat in the center of a circle formed by a hospital, an elementary school, and a couple of cookie-cutter chain hotels. It reminded Burke of the low, squat, rectangular structures she used to build with Lego Bricks when she was a kid. At some point, an attempt had been made at landscaping with rocks of varying size and texture, but no one had done a thing to prevent scrubby high-desert weeds from poking up all over the place. A tattered American flag with the New Mexico state flag below it, flapped in the chilly winter wind. A clip on its rope banged against the hollow metal flagpole, an annoying metronome keeping time for the residents inside who had little to do aside from counting their remaining minutes.

Stanley maneuvered the Cadillac into one of the angled parking places along the street and they all clambered out.

"I got this." Burke took the point position, leading the little group along the cracked concrete sidewalk to the sliding glass doors.

A woman with a helmet of thick black hair and a mask of bright indigo eye shadow peered at them through an open window cut into the plain wall. Half a dozen utilitarian chairs had been pushed up against the walls. A cheap end table held a stack of ancient magazines. The most welcoming item in the room was the bottle of hand-sanitizer which, instead of the standard clear plastic container, sported a poorly rendered evergreen forest.

Burke waited for the woman to ask if she could help them but, when waiting threatened to turn into a staring contest, she produced a badge—yet another item mysteriously procured by Stanley.

"I'm Agent Martin. These are my associates, Agent Bell and Agent Kapcheck."

The woman's gaze darted to Richard, lingered on Stanley, did a slow examination down to his toes and back up, then returned to Burke.

"We were hoping to speak with one of your employees, an orderly by the name of Kenneth," Burke said.

"They're too old to be FBI agents," the woman said.

Burke snapped her badge shut and slipped it into her pocket. "They're not field agents. They're special assist on an investigation I'm leading."

"An investigation about an orderly at a retirement home?"

"No, ma'am. We only want to ask Kenneth a few questions."

"Kenneth is on the clock. We're not paying him to answer questions." Her staccato voice brought to mind the stutter of machine gun spray.

Burke took a deep, calming breath. "I'd be much obliged, ma'am, if you could just—"

The dented metal door to Burke's right burst open and a Native American guy with a braid down to his waist and bags the size of steamer trunks under his eyes beckoned to them. "Come in. Geez. I been hoping you'd get here. I'll tell you everything I know. Just hurry, okay? Geez."

The woman at the desk glared at Burke. "Kenneth needs to clock out while he's talking to you."

Burke leaned in close. "Tell you what, why don't you let him keep the four dollars he'll earn during that time and write it off on your taxes. It's not like you won't make it back in charging the state twelve dollars per pill when you dose the poor souls who have to live under your care with generic over-the-counter laxatives. Or if you want to make a big issue of it, I could call my friend who investigates for the IRS and let him know how tight you like to keep your books."

The woman pressed her red-glossed lips into a thin, tight line.

Burke nodded. "I thought so."

Burke turned and she, Stanley, and Richard followed Kenneth through the door into the interior of the facility. Kenneth glided along the white-washed hallways with long, loping strides. Burke nearly had to jog to keep up. They passed a dining hall with red-cushioned chairs around plain round tables. The smell of stale cooking grease and chlorine bleach hung in the air. A wall of windows gave a view of a stretch of rock and dust that was, apparently, supposed to be scenic.

"They always put lots of windows," Richard mumbled behind her. "Figure it's so you can look out at the world that don't want you no more."

A single figure slumped in a wheelchair doing just that and Burke sent up a silent prayer that when it was her time she'd go fast and with a gun in her hand.

No one else sat in the common areas, and the halls appeared to be deserted. Rows of doors, half propped open, revealed residents that spoke little and moved less. Several of them followed the little parade with sad, rheumy eyes.

Lord, have mercy. At least the place her grandfather had lived encouraged the residents to hang out in a common room and play cards. Of course, that facility had also been infested with soul-sucking monsters, but that was a whole other problem.

At last, they turned into a room with a long rectangular table, eight metal folding chairs, a microwave, a refrigerator, and a metal rolling rack upon which perched a television set that had been state-of-the-art in 1987. Kenneth waited for them all to enter, then peeked up and down the hallway and shut the door.

"You've got to stop them. Stop her. I mean, geez. You've got to help me." He wrapped his arms around himself as if he were trying to hold the pieces together.

Stanley and Richard sat at the table. Burke leaned against the wall facing the door.

"Do you know why we're here?" Stanley asked.

Kenneth nodded vigorously. "You're hunters, right? You've got to be."

"Why do you need hunters?" Stanley asked, not exactly admitting that's what they were.

Kenneth rubbed his eyes and squeezed the bridge of his nose. He took a slow breath, then told them, "I didn't take this job because I like changing old people's bedsheets. It was passed down to me. My family—this is what we do. I'm told it's a gift, but geez." He grunted. "It's a curse, if ever there was one."

"Nathanial told us you keep the spirits quiet," Burke said.

He hugged himself again. "That's the idea. They try to communicate and they get frustrated. Frustrated ghosts are not something you want roaming your city. We can hear them so we let them talk and answer when we can. We have a little authority over them, just because of family history, you know, but right now, geez, things are falling apart."

"You're a ghost shrink?" Richard asked.

"You're a hunter. Are you judging?" Kenneth shot back.

Richard raised his hand in surrender. "Ain't judging. Just asking. Don't get your panties in a bunch."

Kenneth deflated like a week-old party balloon. "Look. You people need to do something. Freaking white people. Geez, you came over here. You brought disease and destruction and death, and you killed just about everyone around here and left this spiritual maelstrom in your wake. Now you brought your freakin' Christian devil and she won't leave me alone."

Burke darted a glance at Stanley who had turned the color of oatmeal left on the counter all day.

"Hold on," she said to Kenneth. "I'm not sure what you're talking about with The Devil. We have no business here with her. We're looking for my ex-husband, Greg. He's just a regular human. Not even a hunter. He's off the grid and Nathanial said you might have a head's up."

Kenneth paced to the far end of the room and back again. "Yeah. Some guy named Greg was around a while back. A week? Two? I don't know, do I? Geez. The days all blur together in this place."

Richard grunted.

"Forget him," Kenneth said. "He's gone, I guess, but the spirits are going nuts. Thousands of them. Hell, millions, I don't know, but they're everywhere, and they're freaking out, and I can't control that kind of power and the freaking Devil, man. She's all up in my grill."

Stanley pushed his chair back and stood. "Can you give us a tour?"

"Why? What good would that do?" Kenneth asked.

"I don't know. Nathanial thought that you would know something about Greg, or that you would know someone who knows something. I'm hoping you'll help us, but in return it seems only fair we help you. Let's take a look around and see if we can't get some answers for you." Stanley lifted his chin. "And if The Devil shows up, we'll do our best to deal with that, too."

Kenneth's gaze darted around the room. "Geez, you're not scared of her? You guys are crazy. You're not regular hunters."

"We're just trying to find a guy," Burke said.

She wasn't about to admit that The Devil scared her just about as much as growing old in a place like Villa Cierto. They hadn't exactly parted on the best of terms after their last encounter.

Kenneth looked skeptical, to say the least, but after a moment's hesitation, he opened the door and led them back into the hall. They took a left and passed through a cold spot so intense their breath plumed into the air. Then the cold disappeared, no more than a figment of imagination.

A tiny woman with a wispy cloud of white hair stood in the doorway to her room. Thick black slime ran from the corners of her eyes like tears made of tar. Her voice sounded like metal rims turning on hot asphalt. "They should have never put me in prison. I ain't no murderer. I ain't never killed a man who didn't deserve it."

Kenneth sighed. "I know, Mike. You've told me, and I hear you. Leave this woman alone." He brushed a hand across the lady's forehead, and she slumped into his arms. A muffled scream faded into the distance. The orderly lowered the woman into a nearby wheelchair.

Stanley tugged a clean handkerchief from his pocket and wiped away the ectoplasm on the sleeping woman's cheeks. "This is what you were talking about?" he asked Kenneth.

"This?" Kenneth smirked. "Nah, man. This is normal. That's what I'm talking about." He gestured toward the end of the hall where a dozen knives jutted out of the wall. "Ectoplasm I can deal with, but geez, flying butcher knives coming out of the kitchen? That's above my paygrade."

"Are you hunters?"

The entire group spun toward the flickering figure of a man in an old-fashioned policeman's uniform.

"Are you here to banish us?" he asked.

"We're looking for someone," Burke said.

The policeman blinked out of sight for a moment, then rematerialized a foot or so closer. The temperature dropped by twenty degrees. The half-conscious old lady in the wheelchair whimpered.

"Are you here to banish us?" the ghost asked again.

"We have no business with you," Stanley said. "But we'd like to understand what's happening here, and we'd like to find our friend. His name is Greg. We know—"

"Greg?" the spirit cut in. "You ought to leave him to his fate. He won't be saved."

A new voice joined the growing crowd. "What in the world is this?"

The group spun again and found a woman in a white coat staring at the knife-handles in the wall. Burke glanced over her shoulder. The ghost had disappeared.

Kenneth pushed to the front of the group. "These people are from the FBI. They're here about a guy that was passing through town a while back."

The woman drew closer. "He came here to Villa Cierto?"

"No. Not here," Kenneth said, but the woman obviously wasn't listening. Her eyes were locked on Stanley and growing wider by the second. She shook her head.

"No. Not you. You can't be here," she whispered. "Not here."

Stanley stumbled back and bumped into Burke. She steadied him with a hand on his arm. "Stanley? Are you okay?" Panic raced through her veins. Stanley had only just come back to them from the brink of death, or maybe sanity—possibly both.

He muttered an apology. "I'm fine."

"You are Stanley Kapcheck," the doctor said. She stood close enough now that the writing on her little golden nametag was clearly visible—Dr. Christine Traverse, MD. Her breathing grew rapid. "What's happening here?"

"Christine." Stanley took a step forward. "I'm so glad to see you are well. A doctor. That's fantastic."

"You know each other?" Kenneth asked.

"I'm not here for you, Christine. You're fine. You're safe. This doesn't have anything to do with...well...I'm here looking for a man—Greg Martin."

"A resident?" she asked.

"No. He has nothing to do with you or with this place."

Goosebumps raised on Burke's arms. The temperature was falling again. She reached into her boot and pulled the iron dagger from its sheath.

"You can't use that," Kenneth said. "You don't understand what it does to them."

Stanley reached for Christine, and she took a step backward. "Don't touch me."

His hand fell to his side. "You're not in any danger," he said.

The old lady in the wheelchair contradicted him. "I wouldn't go that far." Black slime pooled in her eyes and spilled down over her cheeks again, dirtying what Stanley had wiped clean. "We're all in trouble, now."

Burke gripped the knife and spun so her back pressed against her grandfather's and she found herself face to face with the most beautiful long legged blonde she'd ever seen. The blonde's bright blue eyes twinkled as if lit by cold fire. Her full lips curved into a smile. Richard must have sensed Burke's tension. He turned and made a sound like a squeaky sneaker on a smooth tile floor.

"In trouble is my very favorite place to be, y'all," the blonde drawled

"See," Kenneth screamed. "Geez, she's a freaking stalker!"

Stanley maneuvered to stand with Burke and Richard, effectively blocking the path to Kenneth, Christine, and the old woman/ghost.

"She's The Devil, Kenneth. Does it surprise you that she's troublesome?" Stanley asked.

The policeman materialized behind the blonde. Three other forms, less material but distinctly humanoid shimmered near him.

The Devil pouted, prettily. "Really, Stanley? Does it have to be like that? I thought we were friends."

"I've never been your friend," Stanley said.

She sashayed to him, then touched one long finger to his lips. The pink enamel on her nail glittered in the fluorescent lighting. "That's true, Stanley. We've always been much closer than friends. You look good, lover. Better than I'd have thought after...you know. I heard you lost your shadow. You do have a penchant for bouncing back from the edge. I appreciate that resilience in you."

Burke struggled to organize her thoughts. The old woman was possessed and needed help. Stanley apparently had some kind of a past with the doctor, and by the looks of things it was nothing good. Kenneth clearly didn't have things under control with the local ghosts. Now The Devil Herself had shown up. Again.

"Don't you have seven billion other people to torment?" Burke demanded.

The Devil laughed, a gentle tinkling of well-tuned bells that, rung long enough would shatter your bones to dust. "Darlin', right at this moment I can't think of a single one more interesting than what I got in front of me." With her left hand she patted

Richard's cheek. "You've come a long way, baby. It's a real pleasure to see you again."

Movement in the distance caught Burke's eye. Half a dozen ghosts had amassed now. One of them had an axe.

"Guys, this isn't good," she said out of the side of her mouth.

The possessed old lady cackled. "This is the most fun I've had in two hundred years."

CHAPTER TWELVE

Richard

RICHARD WAS HAVING A STROKE. IT MUST HAVE BEEN BECAUSE his vision and hearing were all wonky and off center. He could see the Devil, pretty as a fresh-bloomed daisy on a spring day, and he could hear her silky voice, and smell the delightful scent of roses wafting from her skin. But everything else seemed to be at the other end of a long, dark tunnel. Somewhere far away, the lady doctor ordered Stan Kapcheck to leave the building and the guy with the long hair told her the ghosts were taking over the place. Burke made a comment about fighting with iron and rock salt. Stanley tried to get them all back into the crowded little employee break room.

All the while, the Devil's sapphire eyes stayed on him. "You look upset, Richard."

Upset? I ain't upset. I'm dying. My ticker's gonna pop. My brain's gonna burst. My guts are gonna turn to water and leak right out.

The idea of dying in such a monumentally undignified way right there in front of The Devil seemed worse than the actual fact of looming death.

She purred at him like a kitten and answered his thoughts. "Oh, no, Richard. You're not dying. You are more alive than you've ever been. The hunting life agrees with you. I'd be very interested in seeing how this affects your soul later. I suspect that the old you would have cracked in a moment under the attention of my inquisitors, but now? I bet you'd put up a real fight. I do love it when the humans fight back." She leaned close. "Keeps my job interesting, you know?"

Burke's hands fell on his shoulders, strong and sure. "Come on. We're going back in here for a minute."

They crowded back into the grubby little room they'd only just come out of, and he fell back into the same chair he'd recently vacated.

"Stay out here, Mike," Kenneth told the old lady and the ghost in possession of her, and he shut the door in her face.

Burke and Stanley had chosen to remain standing. The lady doctor pressed herself into the corner as if she were trying to pass right through the wall. Kenneth stayed by the door. The only other one who sat was The Devil.

Dang it! He should have stayed standing. Now he looked like a tired old fool.

The Devil stretched her long legs out and propped her feet, encased in furry white boots, on the edge of the table.

Someone screamed in the hallway.

Burke jumped, but Kenneth held out a hand. "That's just Hank. He died getting beat up and he's been screaming about it ever since."

"Are you really The Devil?" the doctor asked.

The Devil flashed her straight white teeth in a sweet little grin. "I am. And I know all about you, Miss Christine. Or should I say Doctor Christine? You've got nearly as good a story to tell as the rest of these folks."

Stanley stepped away from the wall. "She's been redeemed. She's not your concern."

"Hmm. Maybe," The Devil said, noncommittally.

"Why are you here?" Burke asked.

"I go where the action is," The Devil replied.

"What action?" Richard asked.

"Oh! Look at you, all assertive and curious. Nicely done, Richard." She dropped her feet to the floor and leaned forward, propping her elbows on the table. "So, it's like this." She pointed at Kenneth. "You're in over your head."

The boy threw his hands up and let them fall with a smack against his legs. "Didn't I say that in the first place?"

"Why, though?" Stanley said. "Kenneth's family has a gift that they've used to manage the spirit population in this area for generations. Why is he struggling now to do what has come naturally to them for so long?"

"Because a necromancer has risen to power."

"Excuse me?" Burke said.

The Devil peered at her. "Hearing troubles, dear? I suppose that starts to happen when a human woman reaches a certain age. Things start to deteriorate." Her gaze moved toward Stanley. "Meanwhile those of us ladies who've avoided the human germ tend to stay firm."

A little vein that Richard had never noticed before pulsed beneath the surface of Stanley's pasty white skin just above his eyebrow.

"Who's the necromancer?" Richard asked.

The Devil shrugged. "I'm sure I don't know. I've been telling Tonto, here, to figure it out, but he proves more worthless by the day."

"You're a freaking psycho, lady! I can't go up against a necromancer. I just listen to the ghosts talk. I don't have that kind of power." Kenneth had the same posture as a squirrel who'd just realized a car was approaching at fifty miles per hour.

"Clearly. Here's my suggestion. You all need to work together."

She gestured toward the doctor. "Well, not you. As far as I can tell you don't have any useful skills."

"Leave her out of this," Stanley said through gritted teeth.

Richard's hands trembled against the arms of his chair. Stanley never gritted his teeth. Not ever. He was the coolest cucumber Richard had ever known. The reality of Stanley getting upset caused Richard to get upset. More upset than he already had been. Had he ever been this upset? Probably. It had been a strange year.

The Devil rolled her eyes. "I'm *trying* to leave her out of it, Stanley. But the rest of you need to get your act together and put an end to this."

"Why do you care?" Burke demanded.

"You are becoming the brains of the operation, aren't you? Well, I admit I'd be happy enough to watch these restless spirits eat every one of you annoying little mud-dwellers." She winked at Stanley. "Not you of course, lover. But this necromancer, they're a different ball of wax entirely, don't you see? He's taken a soul from my possession."

"He raised a human from Perdition?" Stanley's eyes widened.

"He has done so, yes."

"He's stronger than you, then," Burke said.

The Devil pursed her lips. "I wouldn't go that far, meat suit." She examined her fingernails. "I want my soul back."

The petulant tone in her voice reminded Richard of the days when his daughter had been young and demanding. Something woke in him that had been asleep for decades.

"Don't you take that tone with her. Last I checked there ain't a person in this room works for you, so you don't get to give the orders," Richard said.

Those stunning icy eyes flicked to Stanley and back to Richard. "Are you certain you know what you're talking about?"

"I know it as sure as I know the pope's Catholic," Richard lied.

Stanley had a shady past and his relationship with The Devil had never been quite clear, but since Richard had cast his lot with old baldy, seemed like the best idea to stick with his choice.

"Ew, the pope." The Devil's lip twitched upward.

Screams intensified in the hallway. The old lady called to them in Mike's voice. "Kenneth, some folks out here want to talk to you."

Kenneth rubbed his face with both hands. He looked about as uncomfortable as a whore in church.

"Anyway," Richard chose to ignore the interruption. "You can't tell us what to do and we don't hunt to serve the likes of hellspawn. We came to Santa Fe to help a human friend and that's what we'll do."

The Devil threw back her pretty head and laughed and laughed.

Burke winced and squinted against the assaulting noise.

Stanley edged further away from The Devil.

Richard turned the volume down on his hearing aids.

When The Devil collected herself again, she waved a hand in Stanley's direction. "He's always telling you that the hunt finds the hunter, right? Guess what, dust babies. You've been found." She giggled. "A friend. That's rich. I see your heart, Richard Bell. You'd just as soon let Greg Martin rot in my dungeons than save his sorry soul from whatever trouble he's brought down on his own head. A friend. Ha."

Richard shifted in his seat, dumb as a doorpost when it came to snapping back at her. Blast if the woman...creature...monster... whatever, didn't twist his brain into a knot.

"Find the necromancer. Destroy them. Return my rightful property. Who knows? Maybe along the way your other little problem will work itself out." She shrugged. "Or not. Maybe Greg Martin will die a bad death at the end of a life badly lived. Who cares? Not any of you."

"I care," Burke said.

The Devil tipped her head. "Do you, Burke? Do you really? Or do you just feel some sort of guilty responsibility?"

The old lady in the hall shouted louder. "Kenneth, you really should come out here!"

Kenneth stomped over to the door and yanked it open. Cold air rushed into the break room, and he staggered back. "Oh sh—"

Something slammed into him and sent him sprawling on top of the conference table.

CHAPTER THIRTEEN

Burke

Burke tightened her grip on the iron dagger she still held in her right hand and raced forward to place herself between the ghosts at the door and the young man laying half-conscious on the table. She sliced and jabbed and received two bursts of light and the stench of sulfur.

"Down," Stanley shouted behind her.

She dropped low, stabbing upward as she did so. Another ghost succumbed to the iron. Three gunshots sounded in quick succession. Two of them found a mark.

The Devil laughed.

The doctor cried.

Burke rolled forward into the hallway to find the possessed old lady pressed against a wall with her eyes wide.

"Things are getting a little wild around here," the demon inside the woman said.

A wavering form bearing a passing resemblance to a Civil War soldier sped down the hall toward Burke. "Keeeennnneeeeeeth!"

Stanley faced the end of the hall where the knives were still sticking out of the wall. Burke pushed herself to her feet and put her back to his. Richard emerged just outside of the door. The hall shimmered and shifted with forms of darkness and light. Some appeared nearly material. Others were no more than the suggestion of a form.

Stanley fired his pistol a half dozen more times. "Take my spot, Dick."

The men swapped and Burke swung left and right like some kind of deranged swordsman, cutting a swath through the endless onslaught of spirits. Something slammed into her chest and knocked her back into her grandfather, sending his shot wild. The bullet pinged off a metal fire sprinkler and whined impotently down the hall.

Stanley was back, kneeling in the open doorway with a small glass bowl in front of him on the threadbare industrial carpet. He muttered and poured ingredients a scattered pile of little glass vials retrieved from God-knew-where.

Richard stumbled back and crashed into Burke. He fired again and again.

"Take your time, there, old man," he shouted at Stanley.

Stanley sliced the tip of his thumb and squeezed a drop of blood onto the pile of herbs and dust. Bolts of purple light flashed like electricity from the bowl into the hallway and a horrible shrieking rose from every corner of the building.

Burke couldn't help herself. The sound drove her to her knees. She dropped the iron blade and clapped her hands over her ears. Something cold wrapped around her throat, and she fought to breathe. Another round of purple lightning zipped past her and the pressure disappeared.

The sudden silence was so complete that, for a moment, she worried that her hearing had been destroyed. Then a scuffling noise came from the room to her right and Kenneth stumbled into the hallway.

"Geez! Geez! Geez, I'm done, you guys. I'm done with all of

this. I quit. I quit being the geez-darn ghost wrangler, and I'm done coming to this God-forsaken hellhole every geez-darn day. I'm done with the geez-darn Devil and every one of you freaking psychopaths. I'm done." He staggered away from her. "Geez. I'm out of here."

She slumped forward and let him go. Who could blame the guy?

Her grandfather pressed a hand between her shoulder blades. "You okay, kid?"

Nope. Not okay. Her DNA hurt. How did things without bodies manage to hit so hard anyway? She took a deep breath, which hurt, and sat up straight on her knees, a movement that hurt, and she spoke, and that hurt, too.

"Yeah. Yeah, I'm okay." She figured she was telling the truth, if by "okay" you meant not-yet-dead.

Richard scowled. "What?"

"I'm okay," she said again. The increased volume passed through her vocal chords like a bouquet of nettles.

Her grandfather reached up and pulled his hearing aid out of his ear. The plastic was warped and steaming. "Dagnabit."

Burke shifted onto her butt and faced Stanley. His skin had turned the color of ash. A trickle of blood flowed from one ear.

He smiled. "I didn't run."

She couldn't help but return his grin. "No, Stanley. You certainly did not."

And thank God for that. If Stanley had still been the shrinking fear-riddled man he'd been a few weeks earlier, there was no doubt she'd be just another ghost in the hallways of Villa Cierto by now.

The Devil squatted behind him and ran a hand over his bald head. "I love it when you work your magic, Stanley Kapcheck." She kissed him, leaving an imprint of red lipstick on his head, then rose to her full, leggy height. "Well, kids, that was fun, but I'm going to run now."

Burke pushed to her feet. "Hold on. You seem to be the only one with any answers. Did the Necromancer raise all these spirits?"

"No. Just the one, but that was enough to make a tear in the veil." She wiggled her eyebrows at Burke. "Let the good times roll, right?"

Burke refused to give in to her desire to slump against the wall behind her. "What, exactly, do you expect us to do? If this necromancer is cloaked from you, how do you expect us to find them? If they're so powerful you can't stop them, what makes you think we can do it?"

The Devil's smile broadened. "Everybody has to have faith in something, dear. I have faith in you. You'll figure it out." She tossed her wavy hair back. "I've got some sources. I'll go check with them and if I find anything useful, I'll come back and let you know." She winked at Richard. "Pleasure doing business with you, Dick."

A person might expect trumpets and fanfare, or at least smoke and hissing, from a creature like The Devil, but they'd be disappointed. She didn't even disappear like a proper magician, she just sashayed down the hall and out of sight.

Burke retrieved her blade from the floor and tucked it into her boot before extending a hand to her grandfather and then Stanley. To her surprise, neither one of the usually prideful men objected to the help and she pulled them to their feet

Stanley faced the doctor still cowering in the corner. "I'll come back, and we'll talk."

"Please don't," she said. "I never want to see you again, or him. Especially not him. Please tell him to stay far away from me."

"He's dead. Busar"—Stanley seemed to choke on the name of his lost mentor before recovering— "Busar killed it."

She shook her head. "No, he's not."

"He's gone. I promise."

She wiped a streak of tears from her cheek. "Gone and dead

aren't at all the same thing, are they? You of all people should know that."

Stanley bent to retrieve the glass bowl, now cracked and streaked with black residue. He dumped it in a trash can inside the break room.

It occurred to Burke that she should ask some questions about the exchange, but she didn't have any energy left to dredge any curiosity out of her emotional well.

"Well, what do we do now?" Richard asked.

Burke took a few steps down the hall and peeked into a couple rooms. The residents were all asleep, streaks of black on their cheeks. She had no idea how they'd made it back to their bed, recliners, and wheelchairs, but apparently being possessed and exercised really took a toll on a person.

Behind her, Stanley answered. "I guess we find a necromancer."

Burke faced him. "What about Greg?"

"What?" Richard asked.

"What about Greg?" she shouted.

"What's wrong with your leg?" Richard asked.

Stanley clapped him on the back. "Maybe the first thing we need to find is a new hearing aid."

"A Nubian blade? Is that how you fight a necromancer?" Richard asked.

Burke told Stanley she thought a hearing aid was an excellent idea. The hunters left the nursing home, only to find another surprise visitor—this one a stranger with curly black hair that hung to her teeny-tiny waist and boobs that resembled honeydew melons.

She leaned against the Cadillac and watched them approach. "I don't know what happened in there, but I have to say, I'm fairly impressed to see anyone walking away from that mess unharmed."

Burke took a mental inventory of her injuries and thought "unharmed" was a stretch. She had a gash on one thigh, her left side throbbed with her heartbeat, and surely some spectacular bruises were blooming beneath her clothing, but she kept that to herself.

"I don't believe I've had the pleasure," Stanley said.

She took Stanley in for a long moment. "I do believe you've had a fair share of pleasure. You're that kind of guy. It positively radiates from you."

"Who are you?" Richard shouted.

"I'm Moonshadow Rising," she yelled back.

"You some kind of a hippie?"

The corner of her mouth tipped upward. "I'm the witch who's trying to kill Greg Martin."

CHAPTER FOURTEEN

Greg

GREG FELT THE WEIGHT OF A THOUSAND EYES ON THEM FOR the duration of their drive back to the hotel. He knew the desk clerks stared. The children swimming in the hotel pool gazed at them through the enormous windows separating pool from lobby.

Stop being paranoid, he told himself. When he looked, no one paid them any attention. *No one knows. Why would they? How could they?*

They had plenty of time to figure something out.

He shepherded Annie Kay into the room and told her to take a shower. She obeyed him without question, staying silent as the grave—*ha ha, good one, Greg!* He barked out hysterical laughter as he sank into the leather desk chair and hung his head in his hands.

The voice of one of the teachers from the ashram came to him. *"Take control of yourself. Your emotions are signs and signals. They do not control you. Treat them as you would a road sign. Acknowledge them and move past. The signs do not drive the car. You are in control."*

"I am in control." He said the words out loud so his subconscious could hear that he meant business.

By the time Annie Kay emerged from the bathroom in a cloud of steam and perfume he'd convinced himself sufficiently that he was no longer trembling and on the verge of being sick.

"Are you mad at me?" she asked.

"No. I'm not mad. I wonder why you did it, though."

She averted her gaze. "I don't know. I just...the smell...and I couldn't...." When she looked up again, tears pooled in her pretty eyes. "I didn't mean to."

"We can't stay in this hotel. It will take a while, but the police have ways of tracking people in this day and age that far exceeded anything you knew in your day. We have to leave."

She took a step toward him. "We can't le—"

"Hush." The word came out harsher than he'd intended, but she'd startled him when she came at him like that. He chided himself for being stupid and stood, then hurried to her. He pulled her to him. "I know we can't leave. I'm sorry I shouted. I'm just really worried about you."

"When you raise your army, no one will be able to touch you. You can protect me from them."

Her devotion made him feel stupid for his fear. "I'm sure you're right, Babe, but I can't even read the book yet. I'll keep working on it, but what I did for you—I told you that was just a fluke." He drew back and kissed her on the forehead. "A happy fluke, for sure, but I'm nowhere near ready to summon an army."

"You will be," she murmured.

"We need to get out of here now. Today."

She nodded. "I thought you might feel that way. There's a place I was thinking about while I was in the shower. It might be just right. Humans almost never go there, and no magic power would sense you there."

Wrapping his mind around her words proved difficult. "I don't understand. Magic is everywhere. I can feel it, all the time," he said.

"Well, yes, your magic is always with you because it's yours and it's connected to death itself and there is no place on this planet that is immune from death, but this place is special."

"Special?" He wasn't sure that was a good thing.

She took his hand and pulled him down to sit next to her on the foot of the bed. "It's so deeply soaked in magic that magic can't be detected there. Think of it like trying to find a blade of grass in a wheat field. It's a place where we'll both be safe. We can stay there for as long as we need, long enough for you to study the book and learn what you must."

In Greg's experience, things that sounded too good to be true usually were.

"You're giving me the hard sell, babe. What's the downside?"

It was her turn to play the parrot. "Downside?"

"Yes, the downside. If we were talking about the supernatural Ritz Carleton we'd be there already."

"What's a Ritz Carleton?" she asked.

"Don't change the subject," he said.

She pouted. "Fine. Yes, there's a downside. This place is perfect. It's safe and it's hidden away. There's someone there who will help us, and he's strong—much stronger than me."

"Stronger than me?"

She placed a hand over his heart. "No one is stronger than you."

"All right, so it's great, but...."

"I know you love beautiful, comfortable places. I'll be honest, it isn't either."

Did he come across like some sort of priss? He could be rugged, if the necessary. "Well, I enjoy fine memory foam as much as the next guy, but it's not like I'm above sleeping on a cheap mattress if that's what's needed to keep my girl safe."

"There are no mattresses," she said.

"What?"

"Or running water. No electricity either, I'm guessing."

A gang of noisy children, no doubt on their way to pee in the pool and generally make a mess of the public areas went screaming past their hotel door, thumping along like a herd of elephants.

"It's an old mission church," she told him.

"You want me to hide in a church?"

"I'm telling you, this is not like any church you've been in before. You'll be safe there, and you'll be able to study the book. Father Sanchez will help you."

Visions of the hipster priest he'd spoken to flashed through his mind. For an exorcist, he'd been a major disappointment.

"Why would a Catholic priest help a necromancer?" he asked.

Her cheeks grew even more pale than usual. "He's not the average priest. He will help you, I'm sure of it, but he may demand payment."

Greg needed a minute to gather his thoughts. Why did life always have to come at him so quickly? He rose and began gathering their things.

"I suppose I can figure out a way to get some cash, but it's going to be risky."

"He won't want your money," she said.

He paused in picking up a shirt he'd thrown over the chair near the window. "What will he want, then?"

She stared at him. After just about forever, the imaginary lightbulb over his head clicked on.

"Oh, he'll want my magic." He frowned. "But I don't have magic, not really. I mean, clearly, I do, but I'm not sure how to use it.

"Don't sweat it," she said, "It's all going to be easier than you think."

Greg couldn't help it. He was sweating it.

CHAPTER FIFTEEN

Richard

MOONSHADOW RISING LED THEIR LITTLE TWO-CAR CARAVAN through the twisting, disorienting streets of downtown Santa Fe. While they drove, Burke fished a hearing aid from the glove box and handed it back to Richard.

He peered at it skeptically. "This the old one?"

"Yes."

"I stopped using the old one because I didn't like it."

"It's hotter than the bat fir," she said.

He frowned. "You make about as much sense as mudflaps on a speedboat."

She yelled at him. "It's better than the one that burned!"

He stuck the crappy piece of plastic in his ear hole. Feedback settled into quiet static that lingered behind the low growl of the Caddy's tires on the pavement.

"You ain't gotta yell about it," he muttered.

Burke rolled her eyes and turned back to the front. He wondered if it would be the right thing to ask about her feelings. Lord, he hated talking about feelings, but he understood that she saw things different, and surely when a girl with bosoms bigger than a matched pair of beachballs shows up and says she's trying to murder your ex-husband, some feelings get stirred up. Staring at the back of Burke's head, a person would think all was right with the world.

Before they all climbed in their vehicles, the witch had suggested they get coffee and no one argued. The kid had never even reached for a gun while they'd talked to the witch. Maybe the right thing was leaving the subject alone.

Before he could sort out a plan, Stanley turned the car into a parking place in front of a multi-level adobe building. The witch pulled her black and silver Volkswagen Beetle in next to them and everyone got out and followed her down a set of stairs to a place that advertised "organic brew and positive chi."

Richard sniffed the air. Seemed like the greater Santa Fe area had a real infestation. "Smells like they got a skunk under the foundation."

The witch looked over her shoulder at him with a raised brow.

"Ain't sanitary," Richard said.

Burke caught the witch's eye and shook her head. "Don't even try. It'll only get more confusing."

Richard harrumphed. "What's that supposed to mean?"

No one answered. Instead, they arranged themselves in a seating area with a red velvet sofa and chairs. A girl about the same size as an eight-year-old with a braid longer than Kenneth's bounced up to them and asked what they'd like to drink.

The witch and Burke both ordered tea. Stanley asked for an iced caramel macchiato—whatever kind of weird sissy drink that might be. Richard ordered black coffee.

"So, you want the cream on the side?" the little girl asked him.

He shook his head. "No, thank you. I'd just like a cup of black coffee."

"Like...espresso?"

Richard scowled. "Just a cup of plain black, brewed coffee.

Folgers. Taster's Choice. Whatever you got. Coffee. Ain't this a coffee shop?"

She stared at him like he was a crazy person, then wandered in the direction of the kitchen without further comment.

As soon as the waitress was out of earshot, Burke voiced what was on all their minds. "So, we followed you here, just like you asked. Are you going to tell us what's going on?"

Moonshadow Rising crossed her long shapely legs and folded her hands across her stomach. Richard noticed for the first time that the woman had situated herself next to Stanley on the sofa. Typical.

When she spoke, her words rolled into the room like smoke from a fine cigar. "First, please let me make sure I have everyone straight." She pointed at Burke. "Obviously, you're the ex-wife. I've heard all about you."

Burke's painted nails tapped against the arm of her chair.

The emerald gaze settled on Richard. "You've got to be the grouchy grandfather. Richard, right?"

"I ain't grouchy," Richard mumbled.

The witch laughed, and the sound reminded him enough of The Devil's black-magic chuckle that the hairs on his arms jumped to attention.

"That only leaves you." Her gaze locked onto Stanley. "Greg wasn't real clear on who you were. I don't recall him ever even mentioning your name, but it was clear that your presence in Burke's life is a thorn in his side."

"I can't imagine why," Stanley said.

She put a hand on his knee, just like they were long-time lovers. "Can't you, though?"

The tiny waitress scampered up and delivered the drinks. She set Richard's coffee down on the low table last, pushing it away from herself with a look of distaste. "Anything else?"

"We're fine, thank you," Moonshadow Rising said. When the girl was gone, she went on. "I don't think Greg even knew your name, but I don't think I asked around for more than a minute before someone connected the dots for me. If you're the man with Burke Martin, you have to be Stanley Kapcheck."

"At your service," Stanley said.

Richard tried to catch Burke's eye to vent some of his frustration with a significant look, but the darn kid was staring straight ahead, still as a statue except for those restless fingers.

"There are some stories about you," Moonshadow Rising said. "Not all of them good."

"I'm an old man," Stanley replied. "We all have our dark moments in life."

"Don't we, though?" She squeezed his knee before taking up her mug in both hands. "So, about Greg." She sipped and closed her eyes, apparently to savor the blandness of a boring old cup of tea.

"You followed him all the way from Colorado?" Burke asked.

"That's right."

"What did he do to you?"

Moonshadow Rising inhaled the scent rising from her mug. "What did you do to you, sister?"

Tap, tap, tap. Burke's nails clicked in answer.

The witch laughed again. "I can guess."

"How do you know Greg?" Stanley asked.

"Biblically," the witch answered without hesitation.

Tap, tap, tap.

Stanley clarified. "I mean, where did you meet him?"

"He was living in an ashram in Colorado, just outside of Denver. I have a shop in town that sells loose leaf tea, local organic produce, stuff like that. Every now and then he'd stop in for one thing or another. We struck up a friendship."

Burke made a noise like a pig with heartburn.

They all looked at her.

"Oh, please, do go on," she said.

"Well, Burke's got the right idea, of course. When I say friendship, I mean the kind of friendship that involves tequila and nudity."

"And blood sacrifice?" Stanley asked.

Richard choked on his coffee.

The witch took the question in stride. "No, not Greg. We were casual. It was fun."

"Oh, Greg's loads of fun," Burke said.

"Isn't he, though?" Moonshadow Rising sipped her tea. "At least, he was at first, but then he got thrown out of the ashram."

Burke snorted. "He denied it."

"And Clinton denied ever putting a cigar south of Monica Lewinsky, but the truth always outs, doesn't it?" She sipped her tea again and replaced the mug on the table.

A group of women in floor-length tie-dye dresses and moccasins fell through the door in a giggling mass. The skunk smell intensified tenfold. It was very distracting. Richard's thoughts strayed toward the fact that the officials really should do something about that. Aside from the smell, didn't skunks carry bubonic plague?

Moonshadow Rising's voice brought him back to the present moment. "Greg loves to party. He enjoys his fine drinks, and his beautiful women, and he's not exactly the Dalai Llama. I think he was a bad influence on the other men."

Burke quieted her fingernails by hugging herself. "Let me guess. You were having a great time. He made you feel like the queen of the world, and he was more fun than a barrel of monkeys. Then, all of a sudden, he was a drain, a leach, a fungus that wouldn't clear up no matter how much ointment you put on it."

The witch nodded. "Well, something like that. And then he turned mean."

"Mean, but not the kind of mean you could really put your finger on. He'd compliment you, but leave you wondering if you were just insulted," Burke said.

"You look gorgeous today. Better than yesterday, for sure," Moonshadow Rising said.

"I'm impressed you're so on top of things after the way you acted last night." Burke held her arms so tightly she was in danger or tearing her sweater with those nails of hers.

Richard sorted through the statements the women attributed to Burke's idiot ex. Richard had never been smart about women. Barbara had the patience of a saint and then some to put up with him, but he'd figured out real early on compliments should be basic and direct.

You look pretty.

This food's real good.

Can't go wrong with short and sweet. Well… it kept the wrong turns to a minimum, at least.

The witch started bouncing her foot in the air. "Still, he wasn't without a certain level of skill in areas important to me, so I let him stay."

"You let him live with you because he's good in bed?" Burke asked, sarcasm dripping from her words like djinn-killing poison dripping from the tip of a bronze dagger.

"Sure. A woman has needs." She waved at the tiny waitress and the girl hustled over with a pot of hot water she poured over the soggy tea bag.

"Can I get a refill, too?" Richard asked.

She frowned at his cup. "You want more?"

"Ain't that what I asked for?"

She took the cup and walked away, shaking her head.

Moonshadow Rising went on. "Anyway, that wasn't the only answer. Greg is charming. He's a fine dinner companion, and while it cost me to keep him, he also had some fantastic business ideas that meant I brought more money in."

Burke's mouth was no more than a thin slash across her face. She'd told Richard in the past that despite his flaws, the man had a head for business. He might do all right for himself if he weren't always blowing his stash on women.

The waitress came back, set Richard's cup down, and backed away from him like he was some kind of lunatic. Ha! If only she knew who they really were.

"So, forgive me for asking, but if you'd found your tentative peace with Mr. Martin, despite his shortcomings, why are you looking for him now?" Stanley asked.

Burke dropped her hands back down to the arms of the chair and resumed the nail tapping. "He cheated on her, of course."

"He did," the witch agreed. "I came home early one day and found him in my bed with my... with another woman."

"How'd you know that?" Richard asked Burke.

"It's what he does," she said. "It's who he is. He's completely incapable of self-control with women."

"I believe we all sympathize with your sense of betrayal," Stanley said, "but murder seems rather extreme."

The witch leveled her gaze on him. "First of all, Stanley, you have no idea how deep this betrayal runs. When we were together, he gave his blood to those spirits who serve me, thus tying himself to me. His debts are mine until that bond is ritually severed, and I had no chance to do that because he ran away."

Richard hesitated with his coffee cup halfway to his mouth. Gave his blood? What in the name of Sam Hill did that mean?

"Did he give it willingly and knowingly? Stanley asked.

No answer was forthcoming.

Burke cocked her head. "There's more."

The witch played with the teabag in her cup for a minute, then scooped it out and set it on the saucer. "He stole something of mine. A book."

"I ain't never read a book worth killing for," Richard said.

"You don't strike me as a man who's read that many books," the witch said.

Richard asked himself why they were hanging out with witches anyway. Didn't they usually kill these freaks?

"This book has been in my family for centuries," she told them.

"A grimoire?" Stanley asked.

"Of a sort."

Burke stilled her fingers and gripped the arms of the chair. "Some specifics would be fantastic."

Three weirdos in period costumes caught Richard's eye. They were lurking around the cackling women at the corner table. The women seemed unaware of them, but he didn't see how they could be oblivious to three guys standing there staring at them.

"It's a book of necromancy," the witch said.

One of the weirdos turned black eyes in the direction of the hunters.

Stanley formed his hands into a little steeple. "Would you say it's a powerful book?"

The witch scoffed. "It's the most powerful collection of necromantic spells ever amassed in one place."

"And what kind of sick use did you put that to?" Burke asked.

Moonshadow Rising's emerald eyes flashed. "Do I look insane?"

See? Richard thought. *I ain't totally clueless when it comes to females. I know enough to keep my mouth firmly shut when they ask stuff like that.*

"No one in my family used the book. We protected it," Moonshadow Rising said.

Richard couldn't help himself. "Protected it so carefully that any gigolo passing through your bedroom could pick it up and run off with it?"

She arched an eyebrow. "You can imagine that, after generations of successful guardianship, I don't want to be the witch who lost the book."

The women in the corner had another outburst, drawing

Richard's eye. The three guys he'd noticed earlier were gone. He looked around the little shop, but they were nowhere in sight. They couldn't have left without walking right in front of his line-of-sight. Then again, they couldn't have come in without doing the same thing. A gnarly little lump formed deep in his gut.

"Perhaps we could help you retrieve the book without resorting to murder," Stanley suggested.

Why in tarnation would they put their necks on the block to get a book of necromancy for a witch?

She held up a finger. "First of all, there's not a chance in Hades that I'd let you retrieve my book and lock it in some hunter's vault."

Oh! Was that the plan? Huh. That was pretty good. Too bad she caught on.

A second finger was added. "Second of all, Greg deserves to die for his betrayal. Maybe if women were a little more assertive when it comes to settling their scores, men like Greg wouldn't feel quite so entitled to everything from our bodies to the food in our refrigerators." She looked at Burke. "Don't you agree?"

Burke sat with one ankle propped on the opposite knee, fingers locked around her knee, looking about ready to burst. She clearly didn't like being faced with a choice between agreeing with the witch or defending her cheating ex-husband.

She was saved when the third finger popped up. "Third, and I suppose the most practical when you get right down to it, he's bound himself to the book. There's no way to take it away from him as long as he draws breath."

Stanley uncrossed his legs and leaned forward. "What makes you think he bound himself to the book? That means he's used it, right? Given of himself to the magic therein."

"That's right." She took a moment to meet the gaze of each hunter and then she laughed. "Isn't it obvious? I can't track him or the book because they're cloaked in death now."

"You honestly believe he's raised someone from the dead?"

Burke asked. "I'll give it to you, he can be clever about certain things, but magic? He's about as magical as a troll fart."

Richard's eyebrows shot up. A troll fart? That was pretty good. He'd have to remember that one.

The witch's head bobbed back and forth rather like a chicken's. "Doubt me if you like, but let me ask you this. You've been in town for...what? Two days? Long enough to feel the vibe of this city. Are you telling me you haven't caught wind of anything weird?"

"The veil is thin in this place," Stanley said. "Everyone knows that."

Richard fiddled with the crappy hearing aid. It made a whining noise like a mosquito. For good money, he wouldn't have admitted to Stan Kapcheck that he knew no such thing, let alone that he wasn't entirely sure what that even meant.

"I'm not talking about the usual Santa Fe hippie culture claptrap." She jerked a thumb toward the noisy group of women.

Richard glanced around. Where had those three men gone anyway? Not likely they all would have piled into the bathroom together.

"I'm saying that if a soul was drawn out of Perdition—"
Burke blinked. "Perdition?"

"Yeah, you know. Hell. Eternal damnation." She pointed at the floor. "Down there."

"I've never heard of a spell powerful enough to free a soul from perdition," Stanley said.

"Have you heard of everything that exists?" the witch asked.

"For the most part," Stanley said.

Friggin' Stan Kapcheck.

"Well, today you heard of something new. It is not only possible that a soul slipped from Hell's grasp, it's certain."

Richard caught Stanley's eye and telepathed the question as to whether or not they should mention The Devil. Stan sat with his hands steepled under his chin. With a movement sly as a weasel in the dark he brushed one finger across his lips in a hushing motion. Richard got the message. Keep The Devil's visit on a need-to-know basis.

Burke planted both pink sneakers flat on the floor and propped her elbows on her knees. "For the sake of argument, let's say you're right. Greg Martin, the most human human who ever humaned, managed to channel the magic in an ancient spellbook and raise someone back to life. What kind of signs and portents are we talking about here?"

When Moonshadow Rising shrugged, her beachball breasts jiggled fetchingly under her shirt.

Richard stared with determination at a sign on the wall that read, *coffee is life*.

"I imagine every restless spirit in a significant radius would feel that kind of disturbance," the witch went on. "Anyone with any magical training who was here at the time would have noticed it—like a tug on their root chakra. The dead will be drawn to the necromancer. They'll pour into the city. They'll trample the living and possess them trying to get to him."

"It'll be the zombie apocalypse," Burke said.

"Sure. We can call it that. It'll start smaller, though. Places that are already haunted will get more haunted.... Know what I mean? Ghosts who've lingered as ephemeral spirits for a hundred years will take on a significantly more substantial form, buoyed by the promise of new life."

Richard looked away from the sign and locked eyes with one of the three creepy guys. The guy shimmered and, just for a second, the brick wall was visible behind him.

Resisting the impulse to scream and make a scene he whispered, "Ghost!"

"Yes. Ghosts," the witch said.

"Ghost!" Richard jabbed a figure at the cowboy who was now grinning at him and was flanked by his two creepy buddies.

Burke jumped to her feet.

Stanley reached for his gun.

The witch peeked over her shoulder and snapped her fingers.

The three ghosts melted into the floorboards like oil into cat litter.

The witch faced forward and crossed her arms. "Still don't believe me? This city is in serious trouble if you don't help me find Greg Martin and stop him, and the only way to stop him is to kill him."

CHAPTER SIXTEEN

Greg

GREG HAD ALWAYS PRIDED HIMSELF ON UNDERSTANDING HIS own strengths and weaknesses. High on the list of strengths, was the ability to understand women. From bits of conversation, reactions to the world around them, and those little tells all humans had that revealed their emotions, he'd figured out that Annie Kay was a regular chameleon when it came to adapting to her environment.

He'd have bet dollars-to-donuts that she was only a little girl when she learned to use her vulnerability to her advantage. A man didn't need to be Sigmund Freud to figure out that she'd changed course accordingly when cuteness turned to curves. It all caused a man to wonder what she'd done to get sent to Hell.

No matter now. She'd been resurrected into the modern world and, setting aside the troublesome issue of her newfound hunger for human flesh, she'd managed to learn about everything from fashion to credit cards. For all that, she continued to underestimate this time and place. He found it amusing that she worried that the proposition of sleeping on the hard-packed dirt floor in a place with no running water would be upsetting to Greg. He surprised her by explaining there wasn't a thing they needed that they couldn't acquire in a portable version.

They passed through a bar where Annie Kay liberated a few wallets from a handful of gullible suckers, and Greg drove her to the more modern portion of the city, where big box stores lined the streets.

Annie Kay peered through the car window, turning in every direction, lest she miss some detail. "Everything in this part of town has a bizarre sameness to it—miles of rectangles with glowing square signs in massive parking lots."

"Welcome to the twenty-first century," he said. "You'll find a stretch like this no matter if you're in New York or Shanghai, China. Same stores. Same merchandise."

Personally, he found it somewhat comforting. No matter where you went, you knew what you were getting.

She flinched when a semi passed as she always did when large vehicles drew near. "Doesn't all that sameness strike you as...I don't know...Not entirely human?" she asked.

"All humans shop at Walmart. The ones who say they don't are lying," he told her, only half joking.

"I met an Italian once. He told me that there are powers ruling over the world who would give just about anything to weed out human ingenuity or artistic expression." She twisted her hair around her finger. "I'd say they've made good progress."

Greg figured anyone who'd been raised in a time when folks viewed humanity as being divided into Christians and savages could only be expected to harbor some superstitions.

He parked as close to the store as possible and dashed around the front of their stolen vehicle to open Annie Kay's door for her. He constantly surveyed their surroundings, hoping that the police hadn't caught onto them yet. Sure, he'd been committing a little fraud for quite a while but now they had everything from murder to grand theft auto under their belts. Dwelling on the murder part caused his mood to spiral toward panic, and panic would cause him to be stupid, so he was trying very hard not to dwell on it.

"She'd have no way to find you here," Annie Kay assured him.

He almost asked who Annie Kay was talking about before he remembered that they weren't just running from the cops. *Don't spiral.* He took a deep breath and blew it out slowly—a trick they'd taught him at the ashram.

He walked toward the sliding glass doors with his hand on her back. Greg didn't argue, but he didn't agree with her, either. He had no idea which of their pursuers was capable of what, and he didn't want to think about it anymore.

The store carried everything he'd hoped for and more—portable beds, lights, a stove, even a flushing toilet.

"Do so many people need to hide in the desert?" Annie Kay said while running her hand over a collapsible aluminum wine rack.

Greg laughed. "People go camping."

"Camping?"

"Yeah, you know. They take this stuff out into the wilderness and live with nature for a while."

"If they have all this stuff, they're not in nature," she pointed out.

"If they don't have all this stuff they have to cook over a fire and poop in a hole in the ground," he said. "They're people, Babe, not animals."

She ran her hand over a silken blanket with a tag that said it was good up to thirty degrees below zero. "Please don't give too much thought to how people ate and eliminated during my previous lifetime. Your opinion of me might drop considerably."

He pulled her close and gave her a long kiss. "My opinion of you is as high as ever."

"Even though I—"

A woman in a green vest approached and asked if they'd like to take advantage of the daily special on wool socks. Greg took a step back and declined the offer politely.

"Would you like to open a credit card and save ten percent?" she asked.

He shook his head. "Not today, thank you."

"Would you be interested in sharing an email address to receive coupons and news of future events?"

Was this some sort of test to wear him down with tedium? "We're wrapping up here. I think we're all set," he said.

The relief on Annie Kay's face mirrored his own when the lady turned her attention to a man in basketball shorts and a puffy Northface jacket. They hurried to the counter where—thank God for small favors—Herbert Grange's credit card worked on the first try. Greg could have paid cash with what they'd gathered up, but it would have taken just about all of what he had.

He tossed the bags in the trunk and turned the car southward. In minutes, they left the last of the city buildings behind them and began the decent out of the foothills into the lower, warmer, sparsely occupied land that stretched as far as the eye could see.

WHILE THEY DROVE, ANNIE KAY EXPLAINED THAT THE MISSION church she remembered had been a fortress, built by the invading Spanish to protect them from the natives who, for reasons unfathomable to those intrepid explorers, seemed somewhat hostile to the arrival of the church's official representatives.

Even after centuries of neglect, the thick adobe outer wall showed no sign of succumbing to the elements. The chips and cracks that had appeared gave it the air of a warrior who'd been scarred in battle, but never defeated. Greg parked the car outside of the single opening—a gate, just a tad too narrow to drive through--and they left everything but the flashlights in the car and went to explore the courtyard.

Hand-in-hand, they gazed up at the building that had once been white and was now painted with a thin patina of red desert grime. Lest the angry locals make it past the outer wall, the church itself was built to be impenetrable. Heavy hard-wood doors with iron bands stood at the top of wide brick stairs. Above the door, a single small window looked out over the barren land. The broken remains of the old glass glittered in the relentless sunlight. Higher still, was the old iron bell, now covered in a thick layer of bird droppings, and above that, a second cross soared into the sky where a hawk circled, casting his shadow over the earth and those poor, unfortunate creatures lacking wings.

"Welcoming place," Greg said. "I know if I'd lived here my whole life and some missionaries suddenly came along and built this, I'd be super interested in joining up with them."

"You would be interested," Annie Kay agreed. "Or they would torture and kill everyone you loved until you *became* interested."

He grimaced. "And they're the good guys, right?"

Annie Kay cocked her head. "I always thought they were evil. After all, so-called men of the cloth were never exactly kind to me, and the women were even worse. But in retrospect, I realize that paying attention to at least a small portion of their teachings would have saved me a great deal of...shall we say, misfortune?"

He took her hand. "That's all behind you now."

A vision of the dead waitress flashed through his mind. No need to bring that up now.

Annie Kay fluttered her lashes at him. "My hero."

His smile felt a little shaky. "So, this is the safest place around, eh?"

"I told you it wasn't going to be fancy."

He pushed his dark, floppy hair away from his eyes. "I can deal with a lack of fanciness, but I feel...." He fluttered his left hand around in the air in front of his stomach for a moment and then let it fall limply at his side.

"What do you feel?" she asked.

"It's like standing with my feet in a pool of electrified water."

"That's the magic. Just wait until you learn how to channel it. It won't feel like being electrocuted. It will feel like *being* electricity."

"How do you know?" he asked.

She raised his right hand to her lips and kissed it, leaving a red lipstick imprint. "Educated guess."

Together, they mounted the steps. Bricks eroded by decades of exposure to the elements wobbled beneath their feet. The shadow of the circling hawk darkened their path for a split second before darting off again. Greg released Annie Kay's hand and approached the old wooden doors alone. It made him feel pretty good to see that his hand was steady as stone when he reached for the handle. Squeaky hinges protested the opening of the long-shut building, and the odor of dry rot and decay rolled out to greet them.

Greg pulled a handkerchief from his pocket and held it over the lower half of his face. "Whoa."

He ventured into the dim interior of the building. A single shaft of light, streaming through the broken window, provided the only illumination. Birds fluttered in the raw wood overhead beams. Small wooden pews in various states of disrepair lined either side of a central aisle. Greg pulled the small flashlight he'd brought out of his pocket and switched it on. The light hit the wall and revealed large symbols scrawled in red paint.

"What are they?" he asked.

Annie Kay gazed up at them in wonder. "Nothing I've ever seen."

Thick layers of dust muffled their footsteps and, as they moved toward the front of the church with slow, cautious steps, Greg noticed that their breath began to plume in the air, despite the fact that it was at least twenty degrees warmer here than it had been in Santa Fe.

Greg's hands burned hot as a coal in the freezing sanctuary.

Annie Kay looked up at him and gasped.

"What is it?" he demanded.

Her voice sounded almost reverent. "Your eyes are pure black."

He grinned. "You were right, Babe. I am electric." He threw his head back and laughed. No fear touched him here, and the freedom was exhilarating. "Come out. I know you're here. I want to see you. I demand it!"

Annie Kay shuffled backward a few steps, letting him take the lead. She fished in her pocket for her own flashlight and switched it on, pointing it toward the altar. Garlands of cobwebs swung in the breeze of the fluttering starling's wings. A statue of the Blessed Virgin looked down from an alcove. Tears of blood stained her cheeks. Saint Peter, too, cried tears that flowed fresh and dripped to the stone floor, rubies glistening upon the grime. Upon the stone altar in the center of the nave, a twisted, melted mass of metal that might have once been a golden cross sent up tendrils of steam.

The ghost of a man Greg could only assume was Father Sanchez emerged from the shadows, looking no different at all from the way he must have when he'd ridden in with the conquistadors centuries earlier. He stood taller than most men. The hood of his black robe covered his shaved head. When the beam of light hit his form, he flickered and disappeared.

"Come back," Greg said, and the ghost did as he was told, taking on a solid appearance.

"¿Quien eres tu?" the ghost asked.

"Speak English," Greg told him.

"I do not know the language of the—" The priest's eyes grew wide. "What magic is this?"

"The necromancer can make the dead do whatever he wants," Annie Kay said with an unmistakable hint of smugness.

The priest studied Greg. "You are a necromancer?"

"Apparently."

"You traffic with the demons?"

Greg held up a hand and laughed. "Well, now, I wouldn't say that. I mean, I just found this book and—"

"He's more powerful than you can imagine." Annie Kay stepped up behind Greg's and clutched his shirt. "He can do anything. He can raise an army and rule this paltry world."

The priest smiled, revealing jagged black teeth. "How wonderful. I'm glad you've come to see me."

A mallet of fear slid down Greg's spine. Sure, Annie Kay could be kind of creepy and maybe she wanted to eat people, but this guy was a whole other ball of wax. Maybe they were safe from the witch in this place, but they weren't safe. His newfound faith in his powers floundered.

"You know, on second thought, you can go," Greg told the ghost. "I mean, it's not cool for me to make you stay here against your will. Sorry for that, by the way. I didn't really even know I had that power until just now."

Did he have that power before now? Whatever energy saturated the crumbling mission pulsed through him like storm surge smashing against the side of a cliff.

The ghost spread his arms and shrugged. "I'm a humble priest. I live to serve." He flickered out of view and popped back up in front of the altar rail. "I am honored to serve you, Necromancer."

Annie Kay pushed Greg forward. "You *should* be honored. You have no idea what he can do for you."

"Oh, but I do have an idea, whore."

Greg chuckled nervously. "Hey, now. There's no need to be nasty."

The priest vanished and reappeared again, only a few steps away now. "I'll be kind to her if that's what you wish, my lord. I'll do that and more. I will help you in any way I can. That's why you came here, right? You wish for my help."

"Well, yes. There's this witch—" Greg began.

"She shall burn on earth and in Hell below," the priest cut in.

Greg shifted his weight from one foot to the other. "Uh, yeah, well. Okay, then. It's just that she's upset with me--lover's spat, you know? She can't accept that it's over and just let me move on."

"I will slaughter her and serve you her blood."

This is the guy Annie Kay thought he should come to for help? Greg shuffled back a step, pushing her with him. "Gosh, thanks. That's super generous of you, but I really don't think we need to go so far. I just need a place to lay low."

"Let him kill her," Annie Kay whispered in his ear.

"What? No." Greg held up his hands. "I think we've all gotten off to a bad start."

"The whore is right. You should let me kill the witch," Sanchez said.

"Really, I'm not comfortable with all the name calling," Greg said.

Annie Kay shoved Greg into one of the pews. "I might be a whore, but at least I never diddled little boys."

"Foul wench. Repent, or burn," the priest snarled.

"I've already burned. I can take it, but clearly you can't, since you've bound yourself to this earth. You wander to and fro, shaking your chains like a monster in a spooky story." She shook her hands. "So scary."

"You are right to fear me, girl."

"I fear no one," Annie Kay spat.

Greg reached for her arm. "Annie--"

The ghost shrieked and Annie Kay flew backwards and smacked into the wall hard enough to crack the ancient plaster. She slumped to the floor in a heap. Greg jumped up and stumbled over his feet trying to scamper along the narrow space between the pews to get to her.

"Leave her," the ghost told him. "I will take her place at your side. I will keep you safe. I will make your desires come true. You want power, yes? Riches? What do you think I brought to the men who built this place? If I could do so much for them while in my meager human form, just imagine what I can do for you, lord, when you raise me to immortality."

Greg dropped to his knees beside Annie Kay. She stirred and pressed a hand to the back of her head. "I shouldn't have brought you here, Greg. I thought you could control him."

"I can." Greg looked at the horrible gap-toothed grin on the robed figure's face and flinched. "I think."

"You can do anything," she told him.

"Yes, anything," the ghost agreed.

He waved his hand and Annie's body lifted into the air and floated toward the statue of Peter at the front of the church. Peter's wooden arms locked over her torso, hugging her back tightly against his chest.

"You can rule this world, but you will need a strong advisor by your side. Surely, you'd prefer a powerful man of the church over a money-grabbing prostitute," Sanchez said.

"I'm not a prostitute," Annie Kay screamed. She kicked her feet up so high, so hard, the wooden statue was forced to take a step back to maintain his balance.

The world tilted in front of Greg, and he thought maybe this was it—the moment he lost his mind entirely from trying to assimilate too many new and absurd ideas.

"The whore is right," the priest said. "You do have the power to raise the damned to life again. Start with me, and I will call those who will help our cause."

"What cause?" Greg squeaked.

Outside, the wind howled against the walls of the mission. A cloud passed in front of the sun, shading the meager light shining through the window.

The priestly ghost raised his arms heavenward. "They know you're here. They come to you."

If Greg's heart hammered any harder, he'd be as dead as the rest of them. They kept telling him how powerful he was, but what could he do? He didn't even know how to read the stupid magic book. This wasn't what he'd wanted at all. He just wanted his ex-girlfriend to know that she'd hurt him. Now there were ghosts and zombies, and his ex-lover was trying to kill him, and where was Burke, anyway? He'd called her for help, but did she come? No. She was too busy floating around the ocean with her grandfather and some other jerk.

Women! His problems all boiled down to women. Women made his life Hell on Earth and now, because of women, all Hell was literally breaking out on earth.

"I'm done," he mumbled. The sound of his own voice fortified him somewhat. He looked at the crazy woman who'd been the most recent one to victimize him, and the freaking ghost she'd tricked him into meeting. "I'm so done. I'm done with all of this. I'll go to the police and ask them for help. That crazy bitch can't just terrorize me and get away with it. This is insane. You're insane. I'm insane!" He threw his hands up. "I'm done!"

The sanctuary was not large. In seconds, he'd reached the back and thrown open the door. The howling intensified and a wave of spirits smashed into him, throwing him to the floor and pressing him down as they washed into the building, screaming and moaning in the misery of death.

"Do something," Annie Kay screamed. "Take control of this!"

"Do shut up." The priest waved a hand in her direction.

Flames burst from the floor under Annie Kay and her wails took on a new level of intensity. Greg crawled behind the last row of pews and knelt there covering his head as he'd been taught to do during the tornado drills when he'd been a schoolboy.

"Sever your power!" Annie Kay shouted, then fell silent.

Greg cowered on the filthy mission floor, no more knowledgeable about how to sever his power than how to wield it. The ghost of the priest materialized before him. He knew because he could see the disgusting, grimy, sandaled feet in front of his nose. He peeked up at the supposed man of God.

"Let me help you, Necromancer. I will teach you how to rule, and you will pay me by giving me life."

It didn't sound like an offer that was up for negotiation. Greg dared a glance at the pale, filmy stream of souls still rolling through the open doors. They passed into the building then drifted upward, gathering around the rafters like noisy cigarette smoke in the world's most wretched bar.

"Okay. Sure," Greg whispered. "Sounds great. Just let me go get my book."

"No need," the priest said. He held out a hand and the book sailed through the entranceway and landed with a thud. He passed it to Greg. "I'm sure you have been studying what to do, but let us begin with the spell you used on her." He jerked a thumb toward the blackened circle on the floor in front of the miraculously unscorched statue of Saint Peter.

Greg choked back tears and pushed himself to his feet. Where the hell was Burke, anyway?

CHAPTER SEVENTEEN

Burke

BURKE DIDN'T CARE THAT THAT MOONSHADOW RISING STOOD five feet away, she refused to take the witch back to Nathanial's house. "First of all, I'm not sure a witch would actually, physically be able to enter his house. I mean, can a person even see the place if he doesn't want them to? That property has more warding than any I've ever seen."

Neither Stanley nor Richard seemed to possess any kind of definitive answer to that question.

She went on. "Even if she could enter his house, should she? I mean, Nathanial's a pretty private guy. I'm not sure he'd want some witchy stranger just showing up on his doorstep looking for dinner."

"I never asked for dinner," Moonshadow Rising pointed out.

Burke rolled her eyes. "Metaphorically."

"Metaphorically, I don't need your weirdo hunter friend's house. I have my own place in the foothills," Moonshadow Rising said. "You can all come. I'm pretty sure it's not warded against old people."

"I ain't so old," Richard said.

"I'm aged like fine wine," Stanley said.

The witch's eyes twinkled and the corner of her mouth twitched. "Indeed, you are, Stanley Kapcheck. Maybe someday I'll take a little taste."

"You're about two pickles short of a barrel, lady, if you think Stan Kapcheck would get mixed up with the likes of you," Richard scoffed.

Burke could have mentioned that Stanley had some sort of weird ongoing fling with The Devil Herself, so she wouldn't be so quick to say he wouldn't get mixed up with the likes of a beautiful woman just because she happened to be a witch. Wisdom counseled restraint, though. They had things to do.

As it turned out, the witch had made arrangements to borrow a house from someone who was out of town. Burke couldn't help but wonder if "made arrangements" meant she'd actually received permission from the owners, or if it was more along the lines of verifying that the family who lived there wouldn't be back any time soon. Her doubts doubled when she saw the place rising up from the mountain like some sort of palace to the gods of the desert.

The sprawling adobe mansion more closely resembled a pueblo village than a single-family residence. Multiple levels sported outdoor seating areas furnished with tall mushroom-shaped heaters. A fountain bubbled merrily in the center of a circle drive, and when they got out, Burke could make out an infinity pool that appeared to be spilling over the edge of the mountain. Steam rose off the surface, indicating working heaters and she wondered how much it cost to keep a pool that size comfortably warm in freezing temperatures.

Moonshadow Rising let them in and they trouped across cream-colored carpet past cream-colored furniture and into a kitchen with an enormous glass-topped table.

No kids in this house, then.

"Beer?" the witch asked from the fridge.

"I wouldn't say no to a cup of coffee," Richard said.

The hunters climbed onto the tall chairs arranged around the dining room table. The witch slid a board covered with cheese slices and bits of meat into the center of table and sat next to Burke, across from the two men.

"Coffee will take a minute," she said.

"Too late to take you up on that beer?" The Devil asked from the head of the table.

They all yelped. Richard choked on the cheese he'd just popped into his mouth. Stanley and Burke both jumped up, drew weapons, and pointed them in the intruder's direction.

The Devil waved a dismissive hand at them. "Oh, stop."

Stanley fired his entire clip into her chest.

Not so much as a wrinkle appeared in her shirt. She raised a brow at him. "Feel better, Stanley?"

He switched clips and holstered the freshly-loaded weapon. "Yes, actually. I should shoot you more often. It's quite cathartic."

The Devil grinned and reached for the cheese. "Sit."

They all plopped onto the chairs, though Burke for one couldn't remember deciding to do so.

"Here's the deal." She pointed at Burke. "The idiot ex-husband you've been looking for is the necromancer."

"I know," Burke said.

The Devil's gaze narrowed. "Well, did you know that he became the necromancer when he stole the book from his lover who happens to be one of the most powerful witches on this side of the globe?"

"Yes."

The Devil propped her elbows on the table and leaned forward. "Doesn't that bother you?"

Burke refused to be the first to look away. "I'm learning to not let Greg's poor choices affect me."

"Are you, now?" She turned to Moonshadow Rising. "Any kind of an ETA on that beer?"

"You told me to sit."

"Ah. So I did. Well, you can get up if you like. I mean, free will and all that. You don't have to do everything I say, now do you?"

The witch went to the fridge and retrieved a bottle of beer, popped the cap off, and set it in front of The Devil.

"Does this mean we're friends now?" The Devil asked.

"I'm weighing my options," the witch answered.

"Huh. Smart." She met Burke's eye. "Greg likes smart women."

"Greg likes all women," Burke said.

"You have a point." The Devil drained the bottle in a single go. "In fact, he's holed up with a woman right now. I mean, not that anyone's surprised, right?"

Richard smacked a hand against the glass tabletop. "You know, I been thinking about it. We oughta just let him sort it out on his own. It ain't Burke's job to save this loser, and it ain't our business to go fetch every time you tell us to. Maybe we should just go...go to...."

The Devil cocked her head. "Go to where?"

"We could go on another cruise," he said.

Stanley looked at Richard as though he'd never seen him before.

The Devil laughed, wrenching shudders from Burke. "You're a hoot, Dick."

Richard scowled. How many times in his life had he declared his hatred of being called Dick? Burke suspected The Devil knew about every one of them.

"I don't mind if you want to go on a cruise." Blue eyes twinkled at Stanley. "I bet that pathetic excuse for a sea god, Ikatere, would be thrilled." The Devil rose and sashayed toward the fridge where she helped herself to a second beer. After popping the cap, she faced Burke. "Not too sure about the security hunk, though. You heard from him lately?"

"I'm not talking to you about him," Burke said.

"You're not talking to him about me, either," The Devil replied. "In fact, I'd wager you're not talking to him much at all. That's how it is with you hunters. You'll follow a lead across the world, but you can't keep a significant other for two weeks in a row." She sipped her second beverage with more restraint than she'd downed the first. "In case you wondered, you should always bet with me, not against me. I never lose."

Stanley tapped his chin with one finger. "I wouldn't say never."

"Yes, well, I don't recall anyone asking about your thoughts on the subject, Stanley." Her heels clicked sharply against the tile floor when she returned to her seat. "So, do you fools want to know where the necromancer is or not?"

"We're capable of finding him without you," Richard said.

"Are you, dear? Because it seems to me like you've done nothing but chase your tails around the city of Santa Fe so far," The Devil said.

Burke felt a deep empathy for Stanley's urge to empty a clip into her. "Are you going to tell us?"

"Are you going to ask?" The Devil asked.

"No. We're not," Stanley said. "No favors. You want to find him as badly as we do, so you offer this information out of your own free will, or you keep it to yourself."

The Devil stalked back to her seat and plunked her bottle down on the table. "Fine."

"Fine," Stanley said.

Burke caught Richard's eye. Was it just her, or were Stanley and The Devil fighting like an old married couple? He gave a little shrug.

"He's holed up in a ruined church out in the desert," The Devil said.

"What church?" Moonshadow Rising asked.

Burke had been so wrapped up in Stanley's drama with The Devil she'd forgotten about the other woman.

"South of here, maybe an hour over some rough roads," The Devil told them.

"No." Burke shook her head. "Greg won't stay at a hotel that doesn't have double-layered sheets. He's not going to camp out in some ancient ruins in the middle of the desert."

"The magic in that place is so thickly layered even I couldn't detect him there," The Devil said. "Seems to me it's the perfect place to hide from an angry witch."

"If you can't detect him, how do you know he's there?" Richard asked.

"The dead have reported his presence," Stanley said.

The Devil winked at him. "It was never your mind I loved, Stanley, but it's a fantastic mind nonetheless."

Moonshadow Rising looked back and forth between the two of them. "Are you two...." She wagged a finger between them.

"No," Stanley said.

The Devil grinned. "Occasionally."

"We're not," he said.

"We will," she said.

"No. We won't."

"We'll see."

Burke rubbed her throbbing temples. "All we're doing here is wasting time."

The Devil sipped her beer. "I told you where he is. Go fetch."

"Angels can be killed," Moonshadow Rising said. "Aren't you sort of an angel?"

"Come at me, Fam," the Devil replied with a wink.

Burke shivered. She hadn't noticed it before, but the high ceilings in the enormous house left the room uncomfortably chilly.

"Let's focus our efforts," Stanley said. "There's...." His attention drifted to something past Burke's shoulder.

She turned to look but saw nothing. When she looked back at Stanley he was on his feet.

"What's wrong?" Richard pushed his chair back and planted both feet on the floor.

Burke shivered again.

It's so cold. Why is it so cold?

She muttered a curse. "They're here."

"Who?" the witch asked.

All three hunters had their weapons drawn now.

The Devil leaned back and propped her feet on the table. "The ghosts."

"What ghosts?" Richard demanded.

"I don't know," The Devil said. "I don't keep track of who's who. Living human, dead human, whatever. There are so many. Like cockroaches."

A young woman flickered into view and disappeared again. A picture frame flew off its hook and smashed into the wall across the room.

"Hey! This is my friend's house," Moonshadow Rising shouted.

The television popped and sizzled, sending the acrid odor of burning wires into the air.

"Oh, spooky," The Devil said.

Stanley fired a shot at an ephemeral form zooming toward them from the direction of the living room. It exploded in a puff of light.

"Why are they here?" Burke demanded. "You said they'd be drawn to Greg, but they keep coming at us."

"The brains, I tell you," The Devil replied. "It's true that Greg's power is waking them, but they sense what you are. If they happen to catch a sniff of that special hunter aroma, they get sidetracked."

Stanley fired another shot and Richard did the same. Two more ghosts, both screamers, disappeared and left Burke's ears ringing. She bent to yank the iron blade from her boot and something cold and black slammed into her, throwing her onto her back. She flailed as she slid across the floor, then came to a stop near her grandfather's feet.

He staggered back and fired a wild shot into the ceiling near Moonshadow Rising's head. The witch screamed and dove beneath the table. Stanley was lifted a few inches off the ground and pinned against the pantry door. He kicked his feet in the air. His face turned an alarming shade of purple.

Burke threw the iron knife, so it flipped end over end, and Stanley fell, landing on his knees a few feet from her in the same instant the dull blade thumped against the wall, then clattered to the floor. Half a dozen spirits began to take form in the kitchen. Another ten or so beyond the half-wall in the living room. Burke used the edge of the table to pull herself up, ignoring a stabbing pain in her hip. An impotent click sounded from Richard's gun.

"Oh, I hate it when that happens," The Devil said.

"Stop this," Stanley said.

"But it's funny," she said.

"Do you want our help, or do you want us to die?" Burke shouted.

The Devil bobbed her head as though considering the question. Richard choked. He dropped his gun and clawed at some invisible force choking his throat.

The Devil sighed. "Oh, all right. Stop this." She swirled her hand in a little circle and the ghosts drew together in a tight group as though captured by a lasso. "Listen up, y'all. You're dead. You've been dead a real long time. You need to accept that and move on."

One woman in particular appeared particularly solid. Her high-collared Victorian Dress smoked as if she were constantly on the verge of spontaneous combustion.

"The Necromancer has called us," she said.

"The Necromancer don't know his butt from a hole in the ground," Richard croaked, still rubbing his throat.

The Devil propped her feet on the table and gestured toward

Richard with her beer bottle. "He has a point. Go wherever it is you're supposed to go before I take you all back to my place and have my way with you."

A single column of light formed and one of the ghosts followed it up into the ceiling, followed by another and another. The Victorian women burst into flames and disappeared into the floor. Three or four of the ghosts just sort of poofed out of existence, and after a moment they were all gone.

Burke helped Stanley to his feet. "Okay?"

He nodded. "Only bruises."

At some point, when Burke hadn't been paying attention, Moonshadow Rising had crept up to the group. "You could have done that at the very beginning," the witch snapped.

The Devil rolled her eyes. "Right, but it wouldn't have been nearly as much fun."

"You're sick," the witch said.

The Devil dropped her feet to the floor and gestured at herself. "Lucifer? The Adversary? Queen of the Damned? Hello."

"I thought it was a metaphor," Moonshadow Rising said.

"Why didn't you do anything? You're not helpless," The Devil asked.

Moonshadow Rising had the good grace to look ashamed. "I can banish a few ghosts, but I've never seen anything like that."

Burke rubbed her temples.

"Can we get back to the business at hand?" Stanley asked.

"Yes, let's," The Devil said. "We were talking about the hot times you and I have had together, weren't we?"

"You were telling us where Greg is so we can help him," Burke said.

"And by help, she means kill," Moonshadow Rising said.

Burke snapped her gaze onto Moonshadow Rising. "I didn't say that."

The witch planted her hands on her round hips. "I've told you how this ends."

Burke thought she should get some kind of Heavenly reward points for not knocking the woman's lights out. "I don't respond well to people telling me what to do."

The Eagle's song, *Witchy Woman*, played a ringtone on Burke's phone.

"Oh, I bet it's the boat cop," The Devil said.

Burke tugged her phone from her pocket and saw that it was Gordon. She sent it to voicemail and faced The Devil. "How do we stop this, once we find Greg?"

The Devil shrugged. "Not my problem. The witch seems to have a plan."

Stanley laid a hand on Burke's arm. "We'll figure it out, Burke, but we need to go. If so many spirits are descending on this town, we can't waste any more time."

She walked over to where her knife lay on the tile floor, picked it up and slid the blade back into its sheath.

The Devil scrutinized her. "I'm not sure why you're so reluctant to kill your cheating ex. I seem to recollect you being rather motivated to swing an axe in his direction not all that long ago."

Burke ignored her. "I'm going out to the car to get the library." As she left the room, she heard The Devil taunting Stanley with a lewd suggestion regarding her fond memories of his car.

"You carry a library around with you in that old jalopy?" Moonshadow rising asked Burke over The Devil's chatter.

Burke pretended not to hear the question. Where had everything gone off the rails? All three of them were whole and healthy. They had a clear objective: drive to Santa Fe, find Greg. Now they were making plans with a witch and The Devil Herself? When did they start working with the monsters? No way this would end well.

Outside, snow had started falling again, soft, powdery dust more like ash than precipitation. Compared to the harsh, cold, wet snow of the Midwest, this didn't even feel cold. Burke leaned against the car and pulled out her phone. She dialed her voicemail and listened to Gordon's message.

"Hey. I guess I missed you again. I hope you're okay. I'm leaving Miami tomorrow. Hope you still want to see me because I quit my job and all." He laughed nervously and a long pause followed. "Seriously, though, I'm worried as hell about you. It took me a good many years to find you. I...." He paused again and Burke waited to hear what he was going to say with her stomach in knots. "It'll be real good to see you again. Call me."

A robot told her to press seven to delete or nine to save. Her thumb hovered over the seven, then she changed her mind and saved it. Did she still want to see him? So much it burned in her like a wonderful fever. It was horrible. She had no idea how to process all her thoughts about Gordon, so she shoved that drama to the back of her mind, tucked her phone into her pocket, and opened the Cadillac's gargantuan trunk.

The box of books was behind the duffle bag full of rifles they'd used in Texas. She'd forgotten all about the guns and promised herself to unpack the bag and double check that everything was clean and loaded again as soon as possible.

She chose the three fattest spellbooks, the journal of a hunter who'd been known specifically as a gifted ghost hunter and the volume of the *Encyclopedia of Magikal Lore* that dealt with the letters A-E and hauled the armful of information back to the little group in the kitchen where she dropped them on the floor beside the table with a thud.

"Time to study," Burke said.

Moonshadow Rising studied the titles for a minute, then reverently brushed her fingers over the cover with an illustration of a Catholic priest being presented with the bones of St. Peter.

"It's important that you stick to the matter at hand," Stanley told her.

"Where did you get these?" the witch asked as if she hadn't heard him.

"I inherited much of my collection," Stanley replied.

The Devil barked a laugh. "Is that the word you use? Inheritance?"

Stanley's gaze flicked to her. "Don't you have souls to torture?"

"One less than I should. Isn't that why we're here?"

"I thought we were here to save the idiot," Richard said.

Moonshadow Rising pulled the thickest of the three fat spellbooks toward herself and sank into the chair at the end of the table.

"We're looking for a summoning spell, one powerful enough to drag the ghosts away from Greg's authority as Necromancer," Stanley said.

"If you can manage that, I can gather the lot of them and pull them back into Hell," The Devil said.

Burke sat across from her grandfather and opened the ghost hunter's journal. "If the witch can call the ghosts and The Devil can banish them, we can talk to Greg and figure out how to undo what he's done."

"I know how," Moonshadow Rising muttered without looking up from a spell for harnessing the power of a lightning strike.

"No killing," Burke said.

The witch shrugged.

Burke reconsidered the phrasing of her statement. No killing Greg. The witch? Well... hunting was dangerous. She might get hurt.

The Devil clapped her hands. "This is fun."

CHAPTER EIGHTEEN

Richard

After staying up half the night with Burke and Stanley, the busty witch and The Devil Herself, Richard dragged himself to one of the bedrooms on the second floor. He stripped to his shirt and underwear and slipped between the sheets into a bed so comfortable he sort of hoped he'd die in his sleep so he wouldn't have to get out again. Thoughts about fighting ghosts and magic spells and Stanley going soft again and Burke getting mixed up with the nincompoop again swirled in his brain like white glitter in a snow globe. Certainly, no chance existed of a decent night's sleep, but the next thing he knew, he jerked awake, his hand reaching for the gun under his pillow before his brain fully understood why.

Stanley was screaming. It was the sound he'd made on the beach in northern Michigan when demons ripped his shadow away from him. Richard shot out of bed and raced to Stanley's room across the hall. Stanley lay sound asleep, flat on his back, screaming at the ceiling.

"Stan!" Richard lay the gun on the bedside table and gave

Stanley's shoulder a gentle shake. He'd sweated through his fancy overpriced pajamas. "Stan! Wake up, man. You're just having a bad dream."

Burke ran in, gun drawn. "What happened?"

"Don't leave me," Stanley screamed.

Richard shook him again. "Wake up, old man. It's a dream. It's a bad dream."

Stanley's eyes snapped open and the next thing Richard knew, he was on the floor and Stan Kapcheck had a knife at his throat.

"Stan, it's me," he choked through terror.

Burke stepped slowly as if she were tiptoeing on wet ice and squatted down next to them. "Stanley?"

Stanley blinked at Richard, then at Burke. His grip on Richard's shirt loosened and he drew the knife away from Richard's throat. Richard scooted back and took inventory. His bad hip was preaching a sermon, but all his parts seemed to be present and accounted for. Stanley stood and tossed the knife on the nightstand next to Richard's gun.

"Everybody still alive in here?" the witch asked from the door.

"We're fine. Go away," Burke told her.

After taking a moment to call Burke a nasty name, the witch wandered off again.

Stanley rubbed his face with both hands. HIs white tee-shirt was soaked through.

"That must have been some doozy of a nightmare," Richard said.

"It was almost half as bad as when I actually lived through it." Stanley took his shirt off and tossed it over the back of the chair where his duffle lay open, then fished out a fresh one and slid it over his muscled body.

Unnatural freak. At a certain age, it was only right that a man's body succumb to the pull of gravity. Stanley passed that age around the time Richard was learning to tie his own shoes, but here they were. Richard with his old man gut and Stanley looking like one of those Hollywood gigolos. Why couldn't Stan Kapcheck do a single thing the same way everybody else did?

"Was it the shadows?" Burke asked.

Shadows? Oh, yeah. The dream.

Stanley placed his hands on his skinny hips and took a deep breath. "No."

"You wanna elaborate about that?" Richard asked.

For a second, he didn't think Stanley would answer, then the old peacock rolled his shoulders back, puffed his chest out and told them, "That doctor at the senior center, I know her." He crossed to the window and looked out at a bunch of nothing. Snowflakes drifted across his reflection, giving Richard a slight case of motion sickness.

"Okay," Burke said. "Did you save her in a hunt? Is that why she was so afraid when she saw you?"

Stanley pursed his lips and shook his head. "Not me. Busar saved her. I told him to let her die."

Richard and Burke stood there like a couple of dummies waiting for him to say more.

"Feel free to drop the other shoe," Richard told him.

"I lived it once, Dick. I just lived it once more in my dream. I'd rather not go into details and experience it yet again."

Burke cocked her head. "Stanley, if this is a hunt we need to—"

"Leave it alone," Stanley barked.

Burke took a step back.

Richard took a step forward. "Don't you yell at her."

"Grandpa, it's okay."

"It ain't okay," Richard said.

Stanley deflated. "You're right, Dick. I'm sorry, Burke. Please, I'll tell you everything when I can, but not now, okay. Not tonight. I'm not...I can't.... Not yet."

Burke chewed on her lip. "Yeah. Okay. We're here when you're ready."

To Richard's horror, tears pooled in the old coot's eyes. "I know. Thank you."

"Come on, Grandpa. Let's give Stanley some space."

Richard tottered back to his room, favoring the leg that didn't want to cooperate since he fell on his hip. In his duffle, he found two ibuprofen and washed them down with water from the shining silver tap in the pristine bathroom attached to the bedroom. Who kept a place like this clean? Half a dozen bedrooms, twice that many toilets—it was a lot of scrubbing. Whoever it was, he'd be willing to bet it wasn't the same folks whose name was on the deed.

Back in the amazing bed, he thought about Stanley and the lady doctor. She wasn't too many years past med school graduation. She must have been just a kid when she crossed some monster's path.

What kind of creature would leave Stanley scared after all this time? Nothing ordinary. Vampires, ghosts, ghouls, swamp monsters—hunting those things was like hunting deer for Stan Kapcheck. The shadow demons left him in sorry shape, to be sure, but it couldn't have been those. When the hunters had encountered them back in November, Stanley hadn't known what they were. Whatever he came into contact with when the lady doc had been a girl, it wasn't that. Then what? And how many dag blasted monsters were there in the world anyway?

He fell asleep and dreamed of shapeless things with fangs and red eyes lurking in the dark, unseen.

MOONSHADOW RISING TURNED OUT TO BE A GIFTED COOK. "Witchcraft is glorified baking," she told Richard when he expressed his surprise that morning.

He wasn't too sure about that. He never once saw his sweet Barbara summon a demon or sacrifice a chicken when she was baking a cake—not even one of those real complicated ones that would get ruined if he stomped around too loud. It didn't seem right to argue with the one handing you an omelet and hot coffee, though.

Stanley showed up in black tactical pants and a clean white tee-shirt and acted like he hadn't nearly cut Richard a brand new smile the night before.

"What's with the getup?" Richard asked. If Stan wasn't bringing up what happened, Richard wasn't going to be the one to do it.

"It's appropriate to the terrain and it practical for carrying multiple weapons," Stanley replied.

Richard smashed up his eggs between his dentures and washed them down with a cold glass of prune juice. When everything hit bottom and stayed there, he told Stanley, "I've seen you tromp through a swamp in wingtips and chop off vampire heads wearing a three-piece suit. Why did you pick this day of all days to dress like Rambo?"

"I find that most flora and fauna in the American Southwest are more determined than usual to inflict injury and death. Thick trousers and sturdy shoes seemed prudent."

Richard glanced down at his wrinkled khakis and muddy trainers. Something to be said for fancy military pants, sure, but a darn good amount to be said for comfort as well.

Burke traipsed into the room looking like a ninja in some kind of stretchy black bodysuit with a utility belt like something out of a Batman comic. He wasn't even going to ask.

"Where's Satan?" Burke asked.

"Always nearby," The Devil said behind her.

They all jumped.

"Can you teach me how to do that?" Moonshadow Rising asked.

The Devil twirled one pretty blonde curl around her finger. "No."

"Can't or won't?"

Richard had to hand it to the witch. She had moxy.

"Hmm," The Devil said and, ignoring the question, she helped herself to a chunk of ham off the plate next to the stove and plopped back into the chair she'd occupied the night before. Her bright eyes honed in on Stanley. "Sleep well, dear?"

"I didn't spend my night skinning people and ripping out their teeth, if that's what you mean," he replied.

"Pity. You're so good at that kind of thing."

"Stanley ain't some kind of sicko," Richard told her with conviction.

"Are you so sure, Dick?"

Richard stabbed a green pepper, suddenly less convinced.

"Stanley's the best man I've ever known," Burke said.

The Devil threw back her head and laughed.

Richard's eggs turned cold and congealed.

"Aren't we gathered here today in front of you-know-who and these witnesses to solve the problem created by the man you vowed to be faithful to until death do you part?" She held a hand to the side of her mouth and stage-whispered. "You haven't known a lot of great men."

Burke's lips pressed into a thin, tight line.

"Am I supposed to make eggs for you?" the witch asked The Devil.

"It never hurts to do nice things for powerful people."

"You're not a person," she said.

The Devil waved the words away. "Details. Anyway, I already ate."

Stanley smirked. "Baby hearts? The souls of innocent old ladies?"

Richard pushed his cold mess of food around his plate. The conversation was making him more and more uncomfortable. "Can we just go do what we got to do and get it over with?" he asked.

"Are you afraid, Dick?" The Devil asked.

He didn't see any point in lying. "Yes, ma'am, I am."

THE CADILLAC ROLLED THROUGH THE CITY AND BEGAN THE long descent out of the foothills at the edge of town. Stanley let the speedometer needle creep up to eighty where it hovered, with no higher numbers to point to, though the car continued to move ever faster. Burke rode shotgun, leaving Richard to sit wedged against the back door with the witch in the middle and The Devil Herself on the other side.

Moonshadow Rising fidgeted. "Couldn't you just teleport there and spare us the cramped car ride?"

"Sure, I could." The Devil blew a bubble from her gum and sucked it back in, so it made a loud pop that caused Richard's crappy replacement hearing aid to squeal.

"Why would she do that, when she can inflict just a little more misery by doing this?" Stanley asked.

The Devil winked at the witch. "He knows me so well."

Conversation was at a minimum. The hum of the wheels half-hypnotized Richard and the swaying motion of the car churned up the breakfast food in his gut, so it took a minute for him to notice when the car slowed and veered right, up an exit ramp with as many holes as a buckshot turkey. Stanley crossed a rusty cattle-guard and took a right onto a dirt trail that cut through the desert scrub.

"You didn't wear army clothes when we fought the skinwalker in Tombstone." Richard had no idea where that had come from. Some part of his brain must have been pondering Stanley's clothes the whole time they were driving. He found it unsettling to think that his subconscious was dwelling on Stanley Kapcheck.

No one answered him, but the temperature in the car warmed by several degrees, and he noticed Stanley glance at The Devil in the rearview mirror. The witch scooted over until she was practically sitting on Richard's lap.

"What the heck are you doing?" he asked, but he'd already seen. Thick tendrils of smoke rose from The Devil's skin.

She smiled prettily at Richard and he struggled not to puke. "Let's not talk about the time you lied to me, and betrayed me, and killed my pet back in good old Tombstone, shall we?" The Devil said.

Richard cleared his throat and determined to keep his mouth shut for the remainder of the car ride.

At last, a white wall rose up out of the desert like a mirage.

Something slammed into the side of the Cadillac and sent it sideways on the dirt track. Stanley hit the brakes and the backseat passengers all crashed into one another.

When Richard extracted himself from the tangle of female limbs and looked out the window, he saw three men in honest-to-God conquistador armor standing in the road.

"You've got to be kidding," Burke muttered.

One of the soldiers stabbed the butt of his spear into the ground and screamed. Sand rose up in whirlwinds all around them, rocking the Cadillac on its springs.

The Devil threw the door open and jumped out. "Hiya, boys."

The three ghost-men staggered back.

"What y'all doing way out here in the middle of nowhere?" The Devil asked.

Two of the ghosts flickered and faded, though Richard could still make out a translucent outline.

"The Necromancer has posted a guard," the third said.

"The Necromancer. Mmm." She sashayed up to the ghost and pressed her hand to his shoulder. He screamed and fell to his knees in a ball of glowing red light.

"Do you know who I am?" she asked.

"Hellspawn," he screamed.

"Oh, no. Hell did not spawn me. I spawned Hell." The red

light grew too bright to look at and the ghost grew ominously silent.

The Devil blew another bubble with her gum and addressed the remaining two ghosts, now no more than shimmering waves above the road. Any passerby could mistake them for heatwaves. "Go tell your master that we are coming, and we'll not be putting up with any nonsense."

The ghosts moved so fast they left streaks of light where they'd been standing.

She climbed back in the car, and they covered the rest of the distance in stunned silence.

HALF THE GROUP LITHELY JUMPED OUT OF THE CAR THE moment Stanley killed the engine. Richard grabbed either side of the door frame and heaved himself into a standing position. He took a few moments to make sure both legs were awake and willing to obey his commands. Aside from the hip throbbing with every beat of his heart, all the parts appeared to be in working order.

Maybe the throbbing was a blessing. *Least I know my heart's still thumping out a regular rhythm.*

Moonshadow Rising had to wait for the Devil to climb out.

At last, they all stood staring up at the chapel. A single ghost —a little boy—sat on the front steps. His dark hair was shorn almost to the scalp. He watched them with wide eyes and said nothing.

"I thought you said every ghost in North America would be descending on this place," Burke said.

The Devil blew a bubble and spun in a slow circle. "You can't see them?"

Richard looked around. He saw a whole lot of rocks, a fair

amount of sprawling prickly pear cacti, and a buzzard looking down on them from one arm of the cross above the building.

A man in a long black cassock appeared in the doorway, and hot wind whipped across the desert. The bird called out and fluttered away, its great flapping wings casting flickering shadows across the hard-baked earth. The little boy ghost jumped to his feet and flew backward beyond the edge of the wide stone steps—literally flew. Richard drew his pistol and held it at his side, taking comfort in the familiar weight.

"I was told you would like to speak with me." The man stepped out of the chapel onto the steps, and his shadow spread out to the west of him. A real man, then. Ghosts cast no shadows.

That thought jiggled something in Richard's brain about shadows and reality and what it meant to be alive, but he shoved it out of the way. No time to ponder life's Great Mysteries at the moment.

Stanley strode to the front of the group and slid his hands into the pockets of the stupid black pants. "My apologies, Father, but I believe you're mistaken. We asked to speak to the Necromancer."

The priest smiled, revealing the worst set of teeth Richard had ever seen in real life. Didn't the Catholic church provide a decent dental plan?

"No, you didn't," the priest said.

"I assumed it was implied," The Devil said.

The priest squinted at her. "I've been afraid of you for a very long time."

"You're smarter than you look."

"On the contrary, now that I see you in person, I'm utterly underwhelmed. I feel a bit foolish."

"Give me a minute," she said

"I assume you've all come here to stop the Necromancer?" he asked.

"That's the plan," Stanley said.

The monk folded his hands in front of him. "I'm afraid I can't let that happen."

Richard was certain something hanky was up with the guy. "Ain't priests supposed to be the good guys?" he asked. "If you don't let us stop him, this whole town's going to be up a creek without a paddle. What's your game?"

"He's dead," Burke said. "Or he was, until Greg came along."

The Devil tipped her head in Burke's directions. "She's the smart one."

"Smart, perhaps," the priest said, "but still falling short of grasping the full picture."

"Why don't you make yourself useful and explain something," Richard said.

The priest's dark eyes settled on him "All right. I'll explain this. The Necromancer you seek is a fool, unknowing of the power he possesses and too weak to harness that power even if he did understand it." He raised his arms and a crowd of spirits flickered into view. "Come, now, my friends, you're stronger than that. *We* are stronger than that. Show yourselves." He clenched his fists, and the forms grew more substantial and doubled in number. "More!"

Another wave of ghosts appeared. Streaks of light shimmered in the air, coming at them like comets through the crystalline blue sky.

"He's channeling the power of the Necromancer," Moonshadow Rising said.

"How is that possible?" Burke asked.

The witch shook her head. "I don't know, unless.... Surely, he couldn't have been so stupid?"

Burke backed toward the Cadillac and drew her Sig Sauer. She chambered a round. "Are we talking about Greg? Because the Greg I know absolutely has it within him to be this stupid."

"He must have brought the book here," Moonshadow Rising said.

"All right." Stanley still stood with his hands in his pockets, looking as relaxed as a man gazing at the sunset off the end of an ocean pier. "Nothing's changed, really. So, we stick to the plan. Moonshadow Rising, everything you asked for is in the trunk. You do your part, we'll do ours."

She edged toward Burke. "Well, yeah, about that."

Richard backed toward the car, tripped over a stone, and almost went down when his hip hesitated to allow his leg to move fast enough to hold him up. One thing he knew for sure, nothing good ever follows the words "about that."

"I lied," Moonshadow Rising said.

Burke fired an iron round at a ghost that got too close for comfort. "What do you mean, you lied?"

"I don't know any kind of a spell to draw these spirits to me. I have a book. I read what I need. I don't spend a bunch of time memorizing stuff."

The Devil spit her gum out. "Do I have to do everything for you people?" She raised her arms straight above her head. "Hey, y'all, listen up. I'm the big D, Lord of the Dead and all that jazz. Come to me."

An uneasy ripple ran through the ghosts.

An uneasy ripple ran through Richard's guts.

The priest laughed. "They belong to me, now." He raised a hand as if in blessing. "My children. I will give you new life."

Richard didn't exactly see what happened next, but before he knew it, the ghosts swirled around them like a hurricane around the eye of the storm. The Devil burst into flames, and the witch was running full-tilt in the direction of the chapel door.

"Don't!" Stanley shouted, at whom Richard wasn't sure.

Burke took off after her. Richard told his leg to go, but it only managed half a step and he went sprawling on the rocks. A cold-clawing mountain of ice pressed him against the earth, entered his mouth, cut off his air, and blocked his vision. He tried to scream and gagged on the chilly filth in his throat.

So this was how it would end. Killed by ghosts, trying to save the city of Santa Fe. Not a bad way to go. A hell of a lot better than wasting away in an old folk's home. And if the ghosts were focused on him, the others might have a chance at breaking through and taking care of business.

He relaxed against the warm earth. The weight pressing him down exploded away from him, leaving a stinging sensation in his back. He opened his eyes and blinked a few times. A tiny lizard blinked back at him.

"Dick, are you alive?" Stanley asked.

Richard rolled onto his back and squinted against the bright desert sun.

Stanley stepped forward, a silhouette in front of the light. "Thought I lost you there for a second."

"I thought you did, too. Why ain't you in there with the kid?"

"I'm afraid she'd torture me for the rest of eternity if I left you out here to die."

It required a monumental effort, but using the car tire and then the hood, Richard managed to heave himself upright. "She's in there alone?"

"No. The Devil and the witch are with her."

Richard harrumphed. "Why the heck are we standing out here with our thumbs up our butts?"

"I was saving you."

"Well, I'm saved," Richard muttered. "Can we get a move on now?"

Stanley smirked in his usual aggravating way and headed off at a speedy trot in the general direction of the church. Richard hitched along behind him like a toy soldier with a broken joint. He noted the shotgun in Stan's hand and realized the stinging on his back must have been rock salt scattershot.

Entering the church was like walking into a boiling soup pot. Ghosts of varying solidity swarmed in the air like gnats on a humid summer day. At the front of the church, the Virgin Mary held Greg in her wooden arms. Burke wrestled with the witch on the stone floor beneath a stream of red light that connected the Devil's outstretched hands to those of the priest.

Stanley swayed as the spirits buffeted him. "We need to get to the altar."

Richard bobbed his head. "Sure. Right past a thousand ghosts, The Devil, and the zombies who seem to be trying to burn each other up, the two women trying to kill each other, and the bleeding, living statues."

Freakin' Stan Kapcheck and his dang fool ideas.

"There's no other way. That's where the book is," Stanley said with a calm that made Richard want to shout.

"Going through all those ghosts is impossible, man." A ghost smacked into Richard. He pulled an iron dagger from his belt and the blade slipped through as easy as a hot knife through butter. "We can't get to the front."

Stanley clapped him on the shoulder. "We must."

Stanley leaned forward, as if fighting the buffeting spirits like a man walking into a gale-force wind and started toward the altar. He dug his right hand into a pocket in the thigh of his stupid army pants and produced a silver cylinder about the size of a soda can. He pulled a tab on one side and rolled it down the aisle. Salt exploded in every direction and the ghosts shrieked and shrank back toward the walls.

The priest shouted, "No!" but his diverted attention cost him.

Whatever weird energy had been held in the balance between him and The Devil slammed into him and sent him flying backwards over the altar. He crashed into the old wooden cross that hung in the front of the room and fell to the floor. The icon creaked and tipped forward, falling in slow motion as it tore loose from the bonds that had secured it upright for hundreds of years. It smashed into the floor, a split second after the priest rolled out of the way. Richard used the edges of the pews like a cane and made quick jerky progress in Stanley's wake.

The witch broke free from Burke's grasp and waved a hand in Greg's direction. "Severus," she screamed as Burke threw her arms around her legs and brought her down to the floor again.

The witch's arm flailed, and a wide gash opened from the center of Greg's chest to his left shoulder. Greg screamed like a little girl in a Halloween house.

The devil jumped over the two women rolling around on the floor and landed before the altar. Thin tendrils of smoke rose from the stone. Richard continued in Stanley's wake, both of them swinging their knives in front of them like Indiana Jones trying to hack his way through the jungle. The priest struggled to his feet, dragging the enormous cross upright with him. He held it before himself like a shield.

"Forget the humans," he commanded. "If she gets the book, you'll all burn in eternity."

The swirling spirits spiraled toward the front of the church, no longer a force to be pushed through, but a sucking vortex, pulling them forward. Stanley leaped over Burke just as she managed a kick that sent the witch sprawling across the floor. The Devil laid hands on the book and was thrown back by an arc of blue light. The ghosts, pummeling her back seemed to have little effect on her.

The priest laughed. "This magic is not for you. You cannot touch it."

She cocked a round hip. "Well, if I can't touch the book and I can't touch you because you're hiding behind that monstrosity, I can at least do this." She raised a fist in the air and grabbed one of the spirits.

Above her head, the ghostly apparition transformed to a young man, barely more than a boy with a sparse beard and short-cropped hair. His brown eyes widened, and he thrashed, his wrist trapped in the clutches of her right hand. She reached up with her free hand and grabbed his hair. Yanking in opposite directions, she split the spirit in half until it burst in a puff of light like glitter being shot out of a smoke machine. The other spirits hesitated, and the vortex slowed.

Eyes on the priest, The Devil said, "I will destroy every one of these souls and send them to a fate worse than my Hell, and when I am done, I will destroy you, too. Perhaps I'll let the angels deal with the one who would wage war against Heaven." She leapt up onto the altar with one white sneaker on each side of the book. Flames erupted around her feet.

Richard took stock of their situation. Burke had reached the statue holding Greg and futilely tugged at the wooden arms. The witch lay motionless where she'd fallen. Stanley stood between him and the Devil. He looked back at Richard and made a little motion like opening a book with his hands.

Get the book. It's all about the book.

Maybe he wasn't the sharpest tool in the shed, but Richard understood that message just fine. He nodded. Stanley took a deep breath and climbed up onto the altar with about the same quickness and grace Richard had displayed as an eight-year-old boy scampering up into tree branches like a squirrel. Flames licked at Stanley's pants, but he didn't flinch. Friggin' Stan Kapcheck.

"Stay out of this, Stanley," The Devil ordered.

"I can't do that."

"Go away!" she shouted.

Stanley staggered back, recovered, and seized her shoulders, covering her mouth with his own. As if by reflex, she wrapped her arms around him and kissed him back. Even the ghosts stopped swirling. Everyone stared at the old man and The Devil.

Get the book. It's all about the book.

Richard limped forward and snatched the book out from between her feet.

"Here!" Burke shouted.

He tossed the book to Burke just as The Devil broke free of Stanley and looked down at her feet. She saw the book was gone and kicked Richard in the face so hard it picked him right up off the floor. He barely had time to register the pain from having his jaw snapped in half before his spine made contact with the corner of one of the benches and he crumpled to the floor. A second later Stanley landed hard on his side nearby. Funny, all he could see was Stanley, Stanley's face, Stanley's eyes. Then he let go, and it didn't hurt any more.

Not so long ago, Richard had stood on the top deck of a ship at night. Black water, stretching in every direction, and the dark sky above, tattered and torn by pinpricks that let light shine through, gave him the feeling that the boat upon which he stood was the only real thing in the universe. Never had he felt so tiny and insignificant. The immensity of the nothingness around him created such a powerful vertigo that he'd clutched the railing as he staggered back downstairs and below decks.

This place where he now stood was bigger, darker, and more remote than that one had been. He stood alone on nothing, surrounded by nothing, pressed down by nothing, floating up into nothing.

"Hello?" he called, but the sound didn't travel because the sound itself was nothing.

I'm not nothing, though. I'm here. If I wasn't here, I wouldn't be able to think about being here.

Whoa. I finally get it! I think, therefore I am.

A tiny beam of light, like the little keychain flashlight Burke kept attached to her purse, pierced the void and he started toward it. Walking required no effort at all. Pain was a thing, and therefore could not exist in this place. It had been a very long time since Richard had moved without pain. He whooped with joy and took a few big leaps in the direction of the light.

Girlish laughter filled the darkness with joy. Richard halted.

He was wrong. Pain could exist here. His heart lurched and pounded painfully against his breastbone.

It can't be.

The circle of light grew and brightened and now there was something—a woman in a snug sweater and a long, poofy skirt that swirled around her legs at the calves.

Determining that he wanted to be closer made it so. He stood at the edge of the circle of light and, from there, he could see her glossy auburn hair and her wide smile that showed teeth she obsessed over keeping white. Her hands twisted into the fabric of her skirt. She'd always fiddled with her hands when she was nervous.

"Hi, Richie."

Tears poured from his eyes, and he felt no shame in that. "Barbara?"

She held her arms out. He ran to her and wept like a child against her shoulder while she held him in her arms and kissed his head. "I know. It's okay. I know. I missed you, too."

Long years of fumbling along as a single parent, terrible exhaustion, lonely nights spent in front of the television, the cold hatred he'd felt when he learned that she hadn't died naturally but been murdered—all of it poured from him in racking sobs that shook him with such force he couldn't stand, and somehow they ended up sitting on the lush green grass in the warm sun. Barbara rocked him just like she'd rocked their infant daughter until all of the pain was spent and his river of tears ran dry.

Memory faded and only peace remained.

"That's how it ended, then? The Devil got me?" he asked.

Barbara wiped the tears from his cheeks with the soft fabric of her sleeve. "That's up to you, Richie."

He didn't understand and told her as much.

"You're not dead, not yet. This place"—she gestured at the great black void that stretched in every direction beyond the little oasis of life and light upon which they'd been marooned— "this is not what comes next."

"What is it, then?"

Barbara's shoulders lifted. "I don't know, exactly. It's everywhere and nowhere, stardust and the center of the black holes. It's not a place, exactly. Not even a time. It's always and never. It doesn't exist."

He ran a hand through his wiry white hair. "That makes about as much sense as boobs on a bull."

The love of his life threw back her head and laughed. "Oh, Richie. You haven't changed at all."

But he had changed. He'd grown old and wrinkled, learned hard lessons, seen terrible things. Telling any of that was out of the question. Even thinking about it felt somehow sacrilegious in this place.

Taking both of his hands in hers, she answered his thoughts. "You're wrong. Look."

He looked down and saw his strong, tanned flesh pressed against hers. Gone were the thick blue veins and ugly brown age spots. "I don't understand."

"I told you. This place knows no time."

"But you haven't told me what this place is. Why am I here if I ain't dead? Why are you here with me?"

She hesitated as if weighing answers. "In the place where you fell, the veil has always been thin. The Necromancer rent the fabric."

"That idiot," Richard harrumphed. "He didn't know what the heck he was doing and now he's got half the ghosts in the southwest flying up his backside." A horrible thought chased that sentiment. "You ain't a ghost? Tell me you ain't been trapped down here all this time."

"No, I've not been earthbound." Amusement danced in her eyes—eyes that did not crinkle at the corners. She'd never been old enough for wrinkles. "You've gotten surly."

"I ain't surly. I just speak my mind."

"So, speak your mind, Richie. Tell me what you're thinking about."

Women were forever asking ridiculous questions about thoughts and feelings. What was he thinking about? Wasn't it obvious? Maybe she just wanted to hear it.

"I'm thinking that seeing you again is just about the best thing that's happened to me in more than half a century."

Barbara pushed away from him and tucked her legs under her skirt. "You can't be serious."

"Well, I ain't yanking your chain for kicks. 'Course I'm serious, woman."

She set her jaw in the same defiant way he'd come to expect from Burke, and he knew a lecture was in the works. "What a load of garbage," she said.

Did he get himself ganked by The Devil Herself just to come to nowhere at all and get yelled at by his wife?

"It ain't garbage!"

She leveled a look at him that would have sent him running to his room, if it had come from his mother. "We had the briefest of moments together," she said.

"They was good moments," he said.

She agreed. "They were, and no doubt about that. You could make me laugh harder than anyone, and when you made love to me, I felt like the most beautiful woman who'd ever lived."

"You are the most beautiful woman who ever lived."

The angry tension melted out of her. "Oh, Richie. You know that what we had was beautiful, but you've had sixty years to build it into a religion in your mind. We loved each other, and that's all well and good, but it's not the only good thing that happened in your long, well-lived life. Richard Bell, you got to hold our daughter's hand when she walked to the bus stop for her first day of school, and you got to hear her tell everything that happened when she got home later that day. You watched her choir concerts and saw her open Christmas presents. You drank beer and played poker and laughed like a crazy man with those boys from the factory. You walked Madeline down the aisle at her wedding and held her little baby girl in your arms."

She studied his face, as if to gauge the reception her words were receiving. "Do you have any idea what price I would have paid for even a single one of those opportunities?"

He shifted. "I ain't saying there was nothing good."

"But you've implied it, again and again."

He got it now. He went south after he died, and this vision of Barbara was given to him to torture him.

She rolled her eyes, just like Burke. "Oh, stop being so dramatic."

"That grandkid's a lot like you," he told her, and it occurred to him that in recent months he'd come to think of Burke, not Barbara, as the best thing that ever happened to him, which was confusing since one couldn't exist without the other. Thinking of Burke caused the faces of every person he'd saved in the past year to swim through his memory. Of course, all of those folks would go on to have children and grandchildren.

"None of that would have happened without you," Barbara said. "You changed the world."

He ran a hand through his hair—hair that was so thick and soft that the feel of it startled him right out of his thoughts.

She climbed onto his lap again and nuzzled right up against his chest just like she used to do in their squeaky old metal-framed bed. "You have a choice to make."

Certain knowledge of what she was about to tell him swelled out of his belly and filled him with dread. "What if I don't choose?"

"Not choosing is a choice. You can come with me if you want. You've lived a long life. If you want to let go, you can, and I promise you have nothing to be afraid of on the other side of the veil."

He ran a hand down the bumps of her spine. "Or?"

"Or you can go back and keep on fighting, keep loving, Richie. Love is the most powerful good that exists. So much more powerful than anyone imagines."

With his eyes closed and his cheek pressed to her soft, fragrant hair, he could almost convince himself she'd never been gone at all. Even after all that time, holding her body in his arms was as familiar and natural as breathing.

"I love you so damn much, Barbara. Some days, even now, I feel like my heart might just crumble and fall into the hole you left there."

Her arms tightened around him, then she kissed him, long and slow and sweeter than honey. When she pulled away her eyes were twinkling again. "I'll be here when the time comes."

There were a thousand things he ached to tell her, but not a single one would rise to the surface of the soup pot of his mind.

"Take good care of our granddaughter. Love, Richie. Do you hear me? *Nothing* is more powerful than love."

She kissed him again. He'd heard of having your breath taken away, but this was the real deal. He couldn't breathe. He strained against his own body, desperate to draw oxygen into his starving cells. Pain burst through him and, quick on its heels, he sucked in air in a great, noisy gasp. His eyes flew open, and there was Stanley Kapcheck, struggling onto his hands and knees.

A FEW MONTHS EARLIER, WHEN THAT LITTLE TWERP TOOK Burke hostage, she'd woken up from a spell and gone nuts trying to fight. Raging against her captors, she'd succeeded in taking a few out, but ultimately ended up in a cell needing someone to rescue her. Richard had played that scenario in his head again and again and came to the conclusion that no one could blame the kid for fighting like a wounded tiger, but she'd have been smarter to play it cool and gather intel. That's what came to him as he lay on the floor, and he chose to remain still and assess the situation.

First off, there was his own self. If he ever hurt in so many places all at once he couldn't remember a time. He reckoned he'd be able to move, but it wouldn't be quick, easy, or graceful.

Second, Stanley looked like roadkill. He was trying, but the old man was out of the equation for all practical purposes. Past Stanley, the witch lay unmoving, dead or knocked out, he couldn't tell. Burke flipped through the pages of the book, holding it up for Greg to see, and Greg, wrapped in his wooden bonds, shook his head, and cried like a baby.

So far as Richard could figure, the priest and The Devil were waging war by throwing ghosts at each other and the ghosts were making a ruckus like a hundred thousand U of M fans sitting in the Big House watching their team lose to Ohio State.

Discarded weapons lay scattered around the floor. These weapons couldn't hurt The Devil. They might push the ghosts back, but they'd serve no real purpose. No way of telling what the deal was with the priest. A head shot would probably take him out, but then again, it might just make him mad. So the only people they knew for sure how to kill was the people they were there trying to save.

Nothing is more powerful than love.

Stanley collapsed, lacking the strength to rise.

Richard swallowed his pride. "Stanley," he whispered.

Stan pushed himself onto his side facing Richard.

Richard swallowed. *Lord in Heaven, help me. I said some things over the years that were hard to say but this one's right up there.*

Eat the frog, Mark Twain said.

Richard bit the bullet. "I love you."

Stanley looked as confused as if Richard had just started speaking Swahili.

"I love you, you daggon prancin' peacock of an old fart," Richard said louder.

Amid the filth and violence, Stanley grinned. "I love you, too, Richard Bell."

Richard latched onto the edge of one of the pews and dragged himself into a sitting position, ignoring the half dozen vertebrae that protested the motion. "I love you, Burke," he said.

Blast it! Tears pooled in his eyes. He started to wipe them away and decided against it. Maybe, sometimes, tears were the most honest expression of love that a man could show.

He shouted to be heard over the cacophony. "I love you, Burke!"

Burke and her idiot ex-husband gaped at him. He braced himself and managed to get all the way to his feet, though he wasn't anywhere near sure enough about his steadiness to let go of the solid wooden bench.

"I love Stanley, and I love Burke. I love them maybe more than I knew I could love anybody. I love my kid, Maddie, and I loved her husband, God rest his soul, because he loved her, and I did a piss-poor job of showing him my love when he was alive."

On the floor near his feet, Stanley strained for the gun.

"Don't," Richard told him. "It won't do us a lick of good. That ain't the way."

The Devil leaped down from the altar and landed with a solid *thump* that sent little whirlwinds of dust up from the floor. "You stop this, Richard Bell."

In his imagination, Barbara watched him from wherever she was. He wasn't sure if he'd really talked with her again, or if his poor, battered brain just dreamed her up. Truthfully, he didn't really think it mattered much. What she said to him—or what he said to himself, as the case may be—was Truth with a capital "T" and that was certain. For Barbara, he ignored the body-wracking fear that The Devil sent spiraling through his bones and imitated his brave granddaughter by squaring his shoulders and lifting his chin.

"I ain't going to stop. I ain't going to stop loving them, and I ain't going to stop telling them about it."

Her pretty face contorted into a hideous snarl. "You're a fool, old man. I will rip your soul from your body and eat it for my afternoon snack."

Richard clenched the cheeks of his backside together and sent up a prayer that he not embarrass himself.

"A man can't stop speaking the truth," Stanley said. "He's shown his love for us again and again, and we've returned it. I love him, too, and I love Burke. They're the family I've chosen, and I've never regretted it."

"And Burke loves that idiot." Richard thrust his chin toward Greg. Pain shot through his neck at the movement.

The Devil clenched her fists and the ghosts exploded—all of them, in a single blinding, deafening explosion that shook something so deep inside Richard he barely had time to turn his head away from Stanley before he lost his guts. The retching was so powerful he fell to his knees again, and his joints crumpled leaving him sitting like a little kid with his legs splayed out in front of him. He couldn't have stopped the tears now if he wanted to, and they weren't just flowing because he was an over-emotional old man.

"Burke loves him, and he loves her in his own pathetic way," he said through tears. "That's why she's the one he called when he was in trouble, and that's why she came."

Smoke rose from The Devil's body. She held out a hand in Richard's direction and twitched her forefinger in a summoning motion. Richard would have sworn his blood started to boil. He heard someone make a noise like a frightened deer, standing in the road, facing an oncoming Mack Truck.

Is that me?

"I do love him." Burke's voice rose above the rushing noise in Richard's ears. "I love my grandfather, and I love Stanley, and I love Greg."

The priest seized the moment of The Devil's distraction and ran toward Burke, arms outstretched toward the book.

"Oh, give up," The Devil said.

The pressure eased on Richard and a split second later the other man staggered and fell to his knees. In a narrow tunnel of vision, Richard saw Burke whispering to Greg.

"Of course, I love you," Greg said.

The Devil screamed. "You think your stupid love-fest can stop me? You think every human I ever tormented didn't cry out in love for some other human? It's what you pathetic fools do. You fall in love, and then you hurt each other, and kill each other, and destroy everything you touch."

"The love is what matters," Richard said.

His eyes fluttered and the scary, screaming creature grew distant and seemed much less scary. Had his eyelids always weighed so much?

When Richard was a young boy, he and the skinny neighbor kid once made a contraption out of tin cans and string. They stood on opposite ends of the yard and played telephone. When Stanley spoke, his voice had the same distorted far-away quality.

"You're not immune," Stanley said.

"You wouldn't dare," The Devil said.

"I've loved you since the first time I saw you," he said.

Immense heat sank over Richard like a blanket covering him as darkness descended.

Stanley released a breath. "I've loved you all along, and you love me, too. That's what you mean every time you tell someone I'm too interesting to kill. It's why you're never very far away, but in all this time you've never destroyed me, even though you've had no lack of opportunity."

Richard didn't hear what happened next. An overwhelming fragrance of roses, tainted with something like rotten eggs registered, and then there was nothing. True nothing, where not even awareness could exist.

CHAPTER NINETEEN

Burke

BURKE SAT SHIVERING IN AN UGLY GREEN CHAIR NEXT TO HER grandfather's hospital bed, watching the steady rise and fall of the heart monitor. Was it some kind of requirement that they keep the rooms at refrigerator temps? Were they afraid that the sick people would get moldy at a pleasant seventy-five degrees? Outside the slightly ajar door, two nurses spoke loudly about a patient awaiting test results from the CDC.

Well, that's just what a person wants to hear, that they're sharing re-circulated air with someone who has some unidentified disease. In the pocket of her hoodie, her phone vibrated. She pulled it out and glanced at the screen, which displayed a message from Gordon.

I'm ten miles outside of town and can't wait to kiss your beautiful lips. Where are you?

Burke clapped a hand over her mouth. She'd forgotten about him. What if he'd been there at the mission church? What if he'd been killed? What if The Devil found him someday? She may have left, but she surely wasn't gone for good. Burke took a series of slow, intentional breaths, slowing her heart rate, diluting the rush of adrenaline. Then she replied.

We're at Christus St. Vincent Hospital on St. Michael's drive.

She waited for the inevitable questions, but they never came. Instead, twenty-five minutes later, Gordon tapped on the door and stepped into the room. He took in the sight of Richard, hooked to wires and tubes.

"You should see the other guy," Burke said.

A sad smile touched the corners of Gordon' s lips. "I can imagine."

She wrapped her arms around herself to still her restless hands. "It was The Devil."

He walked past between her chair and Richard's bed and perched on the wide window ledge. "So, The Devil is real. Should have known there was some bastard behind all the evil in the world."

"She's a woman."

He huffed. "Guess I should have known that, too."

"Hey!"

He held out his hands. "Just saying."

They sat in silence, staring at Richard while he slept.

"Is he going to be okay?" Gordon asked.

"Yeah. I think so. They say he fractured a couple of bones. He did a real number on his bad hip and blew out his knee, but we've got some stuff that will help with all that."

"Must be some good stuff."

She agreed that it was.

"Maybe you should market it," he said.

"I don't think the maker would go for that. He's not the type to sell his secrets. He shares them with people when he feels so inclined. It's the bump on the head that had the doctors the most worried. They say Grandpa was without oxygen for a dangerous period of time. All the signs are good, but they say he'll sleep for as long as he needs while he heals."

"Where's Stanley?" Gordon asked.

"He's down the hall in pretty much the same condition, minus the concussion."

"You came out of it as pretty as ever."

She lifted her shirt and showed him the thirty-two stitches adorning her side.

He frowned. "Your powerful potion is no good for that?"

She covered up, wrapped her arms around herself again and held tight. Love saved them from The Devil. That's how powerful it was. No stronger magic existed in the universe, and how was she supposed to know what to do with that?

"The guys hurt way more. I can deal with this."

"I doubt your pain lessens theirs." He waited, but she couldn't think of anything to say. Or maybe too many possibilities were clogging up her mind and she couldn't manage to settle on a single one. "You could have told me," he said. "Last I knew, you were trying to find your ex, not doing battle with The Devil."

"Found him," she said.

"What was his story?" he asked in a nonchalant voice, but she had the sense he wasn't feeing nonchalant.

"I don't know. I haven't heard it yet. Everything happened kind of fast, and then we were here, and I haven't seen him since we...since they...." She swallowed the bitter lump in her throat. "I rode in the ambulance with Grandpa. I haven't seen Greg. I imagine he's back at Nathanial's place."

Gordon rose and knelt in front of her. He pressed his palms to the tops of her thighs and the warmth from his hands sent a shiver through her half-frozen body.

"Tell me what you need, Burke. Let me help you."

"I need them to be okay. Can you tell me they will be?"

"They're some tough old dogs." He stood and kissed her forehead. "I'm going to find some food. I'm willing to bet you haven't eaten anything."

She wanted to shout,

Don't go out there.
Don't leave.
Don't come back.
Run away from me.
Go somewhere else.
Please stay.
But she remained silent, and he left.

She watched the steady rise and fall of her grandfather's heartbeat on the monitor. Love might be the most powerful force in the universe, but fear was pretty potent as well.

CHAPTER TWENTY

Greg

THE BIGGEST FIRE GREG HAD EVER SEEN INSIDE A BUILDING snapped and crackled in a fireplace large enough for two men to stand in side-by-side. He sat in a huge, squashy chair directly in front of it and let the heat soak into his stockinged feet. Every now and then, from the corner of his eye, he peeked at the giant who stared at him from the kitchen. The man had braided his beard and wiry little sprigs of hair popped out along the length of his plait. At the end of it, he'd tied a shiny red ribbon in an enormous bow. His hair, on the other hand, looked like it hadn't seen a comb in months. It stood out from his head like a bush. A cat perched on the man's broad shoulder and joined his human in watching Greg do absolutely nothing.

Greg was loathe to be the first one to cave into the awkward silence, but he couldn't take it for another moment. "Something I can do for you?"

The giant's ham-like arms were crossed over his broad chest. "Can't think of anything."

Greg shifted to face him more directly. "It just seems like maybe there's something you want to say."

"There are many things I want to say."

"Get on with it, then. Spit it out."

"I'm struggling," the man said.

"Struggling to speak?"

"My friends risked their lives to save you. Burke asked me to bring you here until she could come and sort things out, but I don't like having you in my home. Still, my mother told me I shouldn't say anything if I didn't have anything nice to say, so I've been saying nothing."

Greg rubbed his temples. He hadn't been able to sleep in days, and the pounding in his temples seemed to increase incrementally every hour or so.

"Look, I know what you're thinking," Greg said.

"Are you psychic?" His tone implied that he was legitimately asking.

"No. I'm not psychic. I'm just not an idiot."

"Richard says you are."

Greg snorted. "I'm sure he does. Despite the opinions of my ex-wife's family, I'm not completely brainless. I have a weakness for beautiful women, though. I can't help myself."

"Every man is able to exercise control when he has sufficient motivation. For most men, basic respect and kindness is reason enough. Perhaps you need more."

Greg winced. For a guy who didn't want to say anything that wasn't nice, he wasn't exactly sugar coating his words.

"Perhaps I do."

"So, was the ire of The Devil Herself enough for you?" the man asked.

The cat leaped down to the table, and onto the floor, and stalked from the room, twitching his long bushy tail as if to tell Greg that no matter his answer, it was sure to be a pile of worthless rubbish.

Greg stood and paced to the mantel to examine the collection of rocks, pinecones, and sticks laid out there. It looked like something that would have been amassed by his six-year-old nephew.

"I didn't mean for everything to get so far out of control."

"What exactly did you mean to happen?" Nathaniel asked.

"I just wanted Running Brook to know how much she hurt me when she threw me out. I thought maybe if I took something of hers, she'd get the idea."

Nathanial uncrossed his arms and twisted his braided beard around the fingers of his right hand. "You stole from her to show her how much you cared? That's pretty twisted, mister."

He had to get out of there. Why was he staying anyway? Who was going to stop him from leaving? Burke and the two old farts were in the hospital. Annie Kay was gone.

"I'm sorry I don't live up to your high moral standards," he said.

The man cocked his head. "You said Running Brook hurt you."

Greg picked up a stone that had sparkling golden lines running through it from a grouping on the far right side of the mantel. "That's right. She used me to build up her business and then kicked me to the curb like a dog."

Nathanial's substantial brow furrowed over his dark, beady eyes. "Hold on a second. I thought the witch's name was Moonbeam or something like that? Who's Running Brook?"

The stone clattered when Greg replaced it with the others. "Moonshadow Rising? Man, that girl is some kind of freaky. I wouldn't touch her with a ten foot pole. I mean, not again, anyway. I met her first, but she was crazy right away and her sister was.... I really did care about her. I never thought she'd come after me just because I took a stupid book."

Nathanial crossed the room in three long strides, grabbed Greg by the lapels and lifted him from the floor. "You need to learn some respect for magic, boy. What you did cost lives and hurt people." Nathaniel shook him like a rag doll. "I love those people. They're my friends, so don't you make light for one single second of the role that you played in their pain. Do you understand me?"

Greg could barely gasp out the word "Yes." He stumbled and nearly fell when the giant dropped him.

"Moonshadow Rising wasn't the one you stole that book from?" Nathaniel asked.

He backed away to put some space between himself and the lunatic. "No."

Nathanial held his fingers up, muttering and ticking off items that Greg couldn't discern.

"What's the problem?" Greg demanded.

"I'm realizing that none of us have put all the pieces in the right order just yet."

The cat sauntered back in, glared at Greg, and left again. Greg had never liked cats, and this one confirmed his suspicions that they never liked him, either.

"I'm not the guy to do that for you," Greg said.

"Fill in the blanks, from your POV."

Greg threw up his hands. "I don't even know what that means."

"Point of view. You're not doing a very good job of convincing me you're not an idiot."

He could leave. Get in the old man's fancy car, drive it into town, leave it at the bus station, and start over somewhere entirely new. Somewhere with water and long, warm days. In fact, that's exactly what he was going to do. He stalked across the room, snatched his coat off the hook on the wall, and yanked the door open to find a wall of snow with the imprint of the front door pressed into it.

"Guess you're not leaving just yet," Nathanial said.

The laughter in his voice rubbed Greg like a rubber eraser dragged across the skin. Greg slammed the door shut and looked out the window. From there, he had a clear view of the Cadillac sitting in the well-plowed driveway.

"You're telling me the only bad snow drift on this mountain just happens to be right in front of your front door?"

Nathanial clucked his tongue. "Rotten luck."

Greg scowled. "There's got to be a back door to this place."

"I wish you luck finding it."

"You can't keep me prisoner here."

The cat sat in the entrance to the single hallway and meowed, as if in argument.

Anger leaked out of him, leaving him feeling like a deflated balloon. He tossed the coat at the hook, making no move to pick it up when it fell, and returned to the oversized armchair.

"From my point of view, my girlfriend caught me in bed with another woman. She threw me out, and I wanted to get revenge, to hurt her, to give her a reason to call me, all the things. I was hurt and angry and confused."

Nathanial sat in the chair nearest Greg. The springs groaned under his weight. He withdrew what appeared to be a small twig from his breast pocket and twirled it between his fingers. "Your feelings got hurt when a woman was angry with you for cheating on her? Tell me the truth, Greg Martin."

"The truth is that I've never been faithful to a woman, ever, even when I loved them. I'll bang any girl who'll have me at the first chance I get."

What the hell? Why did I say that? What did you do?

The man started twisting his beard around his hand. "I just asked you to tell me the truth, and I believe you did. So, now tell me the rest of your story, because I have an idea and it's not the most pleasant thought that's entered my mind today."

"I left, and I took the book. I got a ways down the road and started to get this feeling that something was watching me all the time. It was weird, not anything I could put my finger on exactly, but it creeped me out. I started getting the feeling I was in real trouble, and that's when I called Burke."

"Of all the people you've ever known in your life, why'd you call your ex-wife?"

Greg looked again at the snowed-over doorway, at the cat standing guard at the hallway, and he sighed. "She was the only one I thought might help me."

"She's a fine woman," Nathanial said.

Greg couldn't argue with that. "By the time I got to town, I'd come to the conclusion that all of Running Brook's silly talk about witchcraft wasn't so silly after all. I started to believe that she really was a witch, so I started asking around about how to protect myself from dark magic."

"Find any real answers?" Nathaniel asked.

"I heard a lot of nonsense about sage and crystals," Greg said.

"I'da figured by then you'd have enough sense in your head to know that sage and crystals aren't nonsense." He tucked the little twig back in his pocket. "If one witch is out to get you and another prescribes a remedy, you're a fool to ignore the advice."

There wasn't enough ire left in him to fight about it. "Yeah, well, live and learn, right?" Dang, his head hurt like a mother. "Anyway, I guess I might be stupid after all, but one day the book opened itself."

Nathanial nodded as if this was the most reasonable statement in the world. "Magic takes on a soul of its own. It *wants* to be invoked."

"So, I invoked it."

"What happened?"

"I raised Annie Kay from the dead. But she said others had done the same."

"Not one of them with a lick of sense or decency," Nathanial said. "Go on."

Greg was really starting to hate this guy, but he couldn't seem to help but do as he was told. "She said I was different than the others because I hadn't just returned her to her body. I raised her from Perdition and made spirit into flesh."

"Let me guess. She told you she was your willing servant, and you dropped your pants to jump her faster than Jack jumped over the candlestick."

Hot blood burned Greg's cheeks.

Nathanial clucked his tongue.

"I loved her," Greg said, feeling stupid even as the words came out.

"Yes, yes. You loved them all. Tell me the rest."

"Everything was fine for a few days. We were having a great time, but I couldn't shake the feeling that I was a sitting duck. I mean, she said magic couldn't find me anymore, but there's other ways, right? And maybe she didn't know everything."

Nathanial propped a boot the size of a sled on his other knee. "You could have left town."

"But Annie Kay couldn't leave."

"That's the first thing you said that implied you're capable of thinking about someone besides yourself. Maybe you're not beyond all redemption."

The cat hissed from the hallway. Strange, sneaky creatures, cats. He wouldn't be surprised to find out someday that they came from an alien planet.

"So you stayed in Santa Fe," Nathaniel said.

"Well, close to it, anyway. Annie Kay said she knew a place where we could go and there would be a teacher there who could help me learn how to use the book, but by then—" He really didn't want to give voice to what he'd witnessed in the women's bathroom of the so-called fine-dining restaurant.

"Let me guess," Nathanial said. "By then, she was starting to show signs of being not quite as human as you'd thought at first glance."

Greg's face burned. He stared at the fire.

"So, you'd decided to become a full-fledged necromancer?"

Greg let his head fall back against the chair. "No. I mean, I guess. I don't know. I just wanted to be safe and happy with Annie Kay."

"What happened when you got to the mission?"

Images of the ghosts, the horrible priest, everything he'd seen and heard flashed through his mind. He closed his eyes, but that only made it all seem more real, more vivid.

"I don't know. The priest was supposed to help, but when I brought him back something went wrong. It wasn't like Annie Kay. He was...."

"What?" Nathanial pressed. "What was he?"

"Some sort of psychic vampire. It was like he couldn't take the book from me, but he read it through my eyes. But not exactly like that. I can't explain it. It was like I was the Necromancer, but he wielded all my power."

Nathanial let his boot thump back to the floor and heaved an immense sigh. "He used you as a channel."

"I guess. All I know is it went south, bad. Then Burke and the old guys showed up with the Devil and she—" The screams of the tortured souls still tormented his thoughts. "She ripped them apart."

"She's The Devil, Greg. Did you expect she'd be kind?"

Greg looked over at the other man. He wondered if the giant liked girls. With some guys it was easy to tell, but he wouldn't dare hazard a guess about Nathanial's preferences.

"Have you ever seen her?" Greg asked.

The big man crossed himself. "No, and I pray I never do."

"She's the prettiest little thing you can imagine."

"I hear she smells sweet as roses."

Did she? He hadn't thought about it before, but now that it was mentioned, he had noticed the scent of flowers in the mission church. "I'm not exaggerating one bit," he said. "When that woman laughed, my balls crawled right up into my guts."

"She's *The Devil*, Greg. You don't seem to be grasping that."

The cat jumped up out of nowhere and landed on Nathanial's lap.

"Go on then," he said to Greg. "What happened when they all got there?"

Greg held up his hands, helpless. "Chaos. The witch was trying to kill me, and Burke was trying to stop her. The Devil was trying to get the book and the priest was trying to stop her. The old guys were fighting the lot of them—I guess to try to set me free."

"What happened to your Annie Kay?

Greg rubbed his temples. "The priest...he.... I don't know. He banished her or something." The ache in his head increased another tiny notch.

"How did it end?"

"It was the weirdest thing out of a butt-ton of weird things. They all started telling each other how much they loved each other. Burke whispered to me, told me the only chance I had of getting out of there alive was to do the same thing, so I did. I told her I loved her." All of a sudden, it seemed like the most impor-tant thing in the world for the weird giant to believe in his sincer-ity. "I really meant it, too. I know you think I'm some sort of gigolo—"

"Am I wrong?" Nathanial cut in.

"I really do love her."

"Okay."

"Truly," Greg told him.

"Yes, yes. I believe you. So, where'd The Devil go?"

"Well, it seemed like all that love kind of mostly just pissed The Devil off. She got mad. Real mad. But then the bald guy—"

Nathanial leaned forward. "Stanley Kapcheck has done more good in this world than you've ever even dreamed possible. You will address him with respect by his given name."

Holding up his hands in surrender Greg agreed, lest he get his arms ripped off. "She got real mad, then Stanley Kapcheck said he loved her."

"He said that?" Nathaniel barely spoke above a whisper.

Greg nodded. "Yeah, I know, right? He said he loved her, and he said she loved him back, and she freaked out. Like.... I've seen some women freak out, but this one started screaming, and she literally spontaneously combusted. Then Stanley Kapcheck started crying like he just lost his best friend. Next thing, all the ghosts were gone, and everything was real quiet. Then the statues went back to being statues and I was free. Burke called nine-one-one for help. You know the rest from there."

"Not quite," Nathanial said. "What happened to the priest?"

The bacon and eggs Greg had eaten churned in his stomach. "He—"

Nope. Not going to picture it. Not going to talk about those grisly details.

"He died. The Devil killed him, I think, though she never actually touched him."

"And Moonshadow Rising was killed as well?"

"What?" Greg shook his head. "No. Not that I know of. I mean, she was there, fighting with Burke and then...."

Nathanial leaned forward. "Then what?"

"I honestly don't know. I remember the ambulances and police officers. They carried the priest away with a sheet over him and the old—" He caught himself before the giant had a chance to rip his head off. "Richard and Stanley and Burke went in with the medics, and I had the keys so that I could bring the car back here, but she.... I don't know."

"That's not good." Nathanial rose and stomped down the hall and into one of the rooms, leaving Greg to ponder what *"not good"* translated to for him on a personal level.

CHAPTER TWENTY-ONE

Richard

Upon waking in the hospital bed, Richard questioned the wisdom of his decision to stay among the living. Burke sat near his bedside, saying little and patting his arm often, which he didn't hate. When the doctor—some child who appeared barely old enough to be out of college—asked him where the pain was. He thought about it for a long time and finally answered that his hands felt just fine. The boy laughed and told the nurse to inject something into his IV that helped considerably, but gave his surroundings a slightly fuzzy, tilted appearance.

With some hesitation, he inquired after Stanley, and a great weight lifted when Burke assured him that the old prancing dandy was actually faring better than Richard himself. Surgery was mentioned, something about x-rays and multiple fractures and pins and long-term rehab. Richard nodded along, too tired and too stoned to care.

"I'll go see Nathanial and see what he's got," Burke said. "I didn't want to leave while you...." She choked up a little, then all of a sudden, the boat cop was there with his arm around her.

When had he shown up? It occurred to Richard that he must have had one foot in the grave and the other on a banana peel if the kid wouldn't even leave long enough to make the drive to Nathanial's cottage and back.

The two of them must have left then, because the next thing he knew they had returned, and Burke was urging him to roll onto his side which he did with monumental effort before realizing his backside was open to the breeze. Good Lord, did these places allow a man no dignity at all?

She tugged the sheet over him and acted like it was no big deal, but he was pretty sure it was only the drugs keeping him from dying of embarrassment. Then she started massaging Nathanial's healing balm onto his back, spreading it in gentle circles around the fractured vertebrae.

The pain lessened its grip, then let go, and he turned onto his back again and held his hand out. "I got it from here, kid. Thanks."

The doctor walked in just as he was slipping his feet into his shoes.

The boy stopped. "Mr. Bell, what are you doing?"

"I'm feeling much better now. Thanks for the help, doc," Richard said in a stronger voice than a man his age who was looking at months of rehab should be able to speak.

The doctor huffed and puffed like he was the Little Engine That Could. "You can't just leave, Mr. Bell. You were seriously injured."

Richard stood and stretched. God Bless Nathanial and whatever magic he used to make that balm. Experience told him that, in time, the daily aches and pains accumulated over eighty-plus years would return, but at the moment he felt as spry as a twenty-year-old boy.

"Do I look seriously injured to you?" A bout of cheekiness overcame him. "Check it out." Two toe-touches and a handful of jumping jacks left the doctor staring with his mouth hanging open. "Thanks again," Richard said. "Can you point me toward Stanley Kapcheck's room?"

"Mr. Bell, Mr. Kapcheck is—"

"Restored to complete fitness and grateful for your dedicated assistance," Stanley said, popping into the doorway. "Clearly, you and your staff are gifted healers." He slipped his hands into the pockets of his neat trousers. "Ready to go, Dick?"

Didn't seem right that Burke would bring Stanley a well-pressed suit and tie when she only had a clean sweatsuit for Richard. He considered protesting, but he could almost hear her asking if he'd actually want to wear a suit and tie and, frankly, he'd rather face The Devil again. A shudder shook his freshly restored bones. No, that wasn't true. He'd do just about anything to avoid doing that again. Anyway, the clothes didn't seem worth fighting about, and now that he was feeling better, he had a hankering for one of them big Classic Buttery Jack burgers from Jack in the Box.

In the car, Burke broke the news. "I'm glad you're both feeling better, but Nathanial says you've got to hold yourselves together for a while. That stuff can only be made a little bit at a time, and only when the stars are aligned or some such thing, and you just used up the last of it."

"This'll hold me." Richard wiggled back and forth in his seat, enjoying the fluid motion of his joints.

Stanley eased the Cadillac out of the parking lot and turned north, toward Nathanial's house, and asked, "What do we know, Burke? Fill us in while we drive."

Richard laced his fingers together and stretched them out in front of himself, so his knuckles cracked with a satisfying *pop*. "We sent that scary tramp back where she came from, saved the city, and rescued the crying little girl." He chuckled. "Greg, I mean."

Burke rolled her eyes. "Yeah, I got that, thanks."

The landscape around them looked familiar, and Richard's

grin faltered when he realized the building to their left was Villa Cierto. Thankfully, Stanley hit the gas and they zoomed past a good ten miles per hour faster than the signs suggested.

"So, it's like this," Burke leaned over the back of the front seat so that her head was between Richard's and Stanley's, "Nathanial got Greg to spill his guts about everything that happened from the start."

The smidge of grin remaining on Richard's face died. Bad news was on the way—just when he'd been feeling so darn good, too. Wasn't that always the way? Life's unfairness knew no bounds.

Burke explained that not only was the witch in the wind, but she'd lied about who she was. Not Greg's ex-lover, Running Brook, but Running Brook's sister. "We don't know where Moonshadow Rising is, and we don't know what shape she's in or what she's planning to do next."

"Running Brook? They Indian girls?" Richard asked. "The other one didn't look Indian to me."

"Native American," Burke said.

Richard nodded. "Yeah. Like that."

Burke sighed. "Grandpa, I.... Nevermind. I think they just had hippie parents."

Dang hippie weirdos. He hadn't liked them in 1968, and he didn't like them now.

Houses grew fewer and farther between, and the snow piles on the sides of the road grew deeper as they climbed higher into the mountains.

Richard remembered that he'd wanted to stop at Jack in the Box. Dang it! He forgot to say something while they were in town and now there'd be no getting them to go back. May as well stick to the topic.

"Well, she's gone, now, so we're in the clear, right?" he said.

Neither of the others answered him, and they drove in silence the rest of the way to Nathanial's cottage.

CHAPTER TWENTY-TWO

Burke

THE CADILLAC SLID TO A STOP ON TOP OF SNOW THAT HAD BEEN melted by the movement of vehicles and re-frozen overnight. Stanley reached for the door handle and Burke stopped him.

"There's something I need to ask you guys."

Both men twisted around to peer over the back of the seat at her.

A muddled mess of thoughts and feelings swirled in the chaos of her thoughts. What did she want to ask, really? They both knew Gordon and seemed to like him well enough. Neither of them had ever counseled her against the match. Why did relationships have to be so hard? Why were her thoughts such a tangled disaster?

Stanley shifted in his seat, so he faced her more squarely. "Are you all right, my dear?"

What to say to that?

Help me. What would you do?

Would the man who recently professed his love to Evil Incarnate have good wisdom to share? Uncertain as to which words would pop out, she opened her mouth and told him, "I'm scared as hell."

He reached over the seat back, took her hand in his own, and gave a gentle squeeze.

"What if it all goes south?" she asked.

"Oh, my dear, but what if it doesn't?"

Memories of a disastrous marriage plagued her. She blinked away tears. She'd shed too many tears over Greg. He didn't deserve any more.

"I have really bad luck with men."

"All men aren't like Greg," Stanley pointed out.

"There was Albert, too."

Richard harrumphed. "Albert wasn't a man. He was a pawn in a game, and that was the highlight of his life. Scrawny little twerp wouldn't have been able to find his own butt with both hands and a flashlight, let alone figure out how to treat a woman."

"I guess I was a pawn too, then," Burke said.

Stanley squeezed her hand again. "Aren't we all?"

She wondered if Stanley regretted being single all his long life. Hunting didn't exactly lend itself to romance. Then again, he seemed to have had his fair share of romances, they just never lasted long. Or did they? How long had his weird love/hate relationship with The Devil been going on, anyway? What did she really know about the century and a half that Stanley had walked the earth?

"You told her you love her," Burke said.

He released her hand and picked a tiny piece of lint from his sleeve. "I do." His gaze roamed the forest around them before he looked her in the eye. "When I was a young man, I had no idea how closely related passionate love was to passionate hatred. It's all rather confusing at times, but one thing I've learned in this unnaturally long life, is that the opposite of love is not hate, but indifference."

Countless fantasies of maiming Greg had flashed through her mind over the years. She understood what Stanley was saying.

"I think you're right, but I don't want to hate Gordon. I don't even want to risk it."

Stanley shrugged. "Then you risk never loving him. Are you willing to live with that? When you look back on this moment, twenty years from now, will you be grateful that you chose safety? It's a wise woman who moves through life with caution and awareness, but there's a fine line between caution and fear. Nothing good has ever come to anyone who was ruled by fear. Everything worth having lies on the other side of fear."

They sat for a time with no urgent need to speak. Burke thought about what it had felt like to be loved by Greg. She'd been the most beautiful woman on earth when his gaze fell on her. When his gaze fell upon someone else, she'd had no worth at all in her own mind. Stanley arrived in her life and changed everything. She learned how to live as the woman she'd always been, and she liked herself. Was *that* the woman that Gordon fell in love with, or did he love some image of her that only existed in his own mind, as Greg had?

And there were other things to consider. "What if he's killed because I brought him into this life?"

"A question I ask myself every time the two of us hunt together, my dear one," Stanley said.

Burke sighed. Bigger problems begged her attention. Her love life was going to have to take a back seat. She reached for the handle and pushed the door open. "Thanks for talking about all this with me."

"Burke," Richard said, and she stopped and leaned back into the car again. "I ain't as smart as you, and I ain't as witty as Stan. I've loved, though, and I've lost."

"Better to have loved and lost than never to have loved at all?" she asked a little sadly.

"So much better I don't even know how to put it into words," he replied softly.

It wasn't very often her grandfather surprised her, but she hadn't expected any such declaration from the man who hated to talk about feelings.

"Your grandmother told me there's nothing in the world more powerful than love. Nothing in the whole universe, is what I think." He pulled the hearing aid out of his ear, and it squealed. He poked it back in, fiddled for a moment, and went on. "Besides, I don't think you really ever lose, if you love. Love is forever. Longer than us. Longer than life. Longer than earth. Maybe even longer than Heaven and Hell."

Words couldn't force their way through the tiny, constricted space in her throat. She climbed the rest of the way out of the car.

Stanley strode alongside her, steady as a polar bear on the ice. "You've come to your decision, then?"

"Nope. Not remotely, but we've got a job to do."

"So we do," he agreed.

IN ABOUT A FOUR-FOOT AREA AROUND THE COTTAGE DOOR, daisies bloomed amid thick green grass. A blue and orange butterfly languidly opened and closed its wings as it perched upon an ivy leaf. The door popped opened, and Nathanial stepped back.

He waved them inside. "Come in, come in! It's wintertime out there and not fit for lingering. Well, mostly winter. We had an unexpected drift at the front door that needed dealing with."

"Most people would have used a shovel," Burke teased as she stepped past him and shrugged out of her coat.

"I'm guessing I'm not much like most people, but I really don't know for sure. I've only met a few."

"You are one of a kind, my friend," Stanley told him.

Gordon leaned against the stone fireplace, a mug in his hands that read, *coffee makes me feel less murdery*. His gaze caressed her as she knew his hands could, warming her up from the inside out.

Greg sat in the big chair directly in front of the fire. He jumped to his feet when he saw her. "Babe, I—"

"Don't." She held up a hand to stop him.

She took her time kicking off her wet shoes, pouring herself a cup of coffee, and pulling a chair over to where the others had arranged themselves.

Richard emerged from the hallway with a spring in his step. "Thank you for the use of your facilities, Nate, and thank you for this hot, strong brew, and thank you most of all for that fantastic medicine."

"Hope you don't need it again any time too soon," Nathanial said. "What I had is yours. You boys have been running through it faster than I'd have expected. Hard to keep up with you sometimes. Even if I could make more, it's best you take a break. Nature isn't fond of being bent to the will of men too often."

Stanley held his feet toward the fire. "We're boys no longer, but old men who ask too much of aging bodies, and sometimes too much of our friends. Thank you for coming through when we needed you."

"Just keep my words in mind. There's things I can do, but rushing Mother Earth's timing isn't one of them," Nathaniel replied.

"Says the man with daisies and green grass growing outside his door in the middle of winter in the high desert," Burke teased.

Nathanial waved her words away. "Parlor tricks, nothing more."

Burke ignored Gordon's gaze with determination.

Later. She'd sort it all out later. Right now, they needed to figure out exactly what Greg had done and whether or not there was still a witch on the loose who could very well try to kill them all.

She faced her ex-husband and spoke careful words, keeping a tight rein on her tongue, lest threats of bodily harm fly forth. "When I asked you if you'd been kicked out of the ashram, you said you left voluntarily."

Greg leaned forward and spoke with his hands out as though making an offering to her. "Yes, but I—"

"And when I asked you if this all had to do with a woman, you told me that it did not."

"Well, you can't blame—"

"You said you did nothing," she cut in, "so far as you knew, to bring this on yourself."

"I didn't mean that I"—he scooted to the edge of his chair, imploring her.

"So, if you lie every time you open your mouth, how are we supposed to trust that anything you tell us is the truth?" she asked.

Greg scooted back again and slumped, his hands limp in his lap. "I messed up."

"Ha!" Richard slurped from his *World's Best Cheerleader* cup, then thumped the cup down on a little side table. "That's the daggone understatement of the century."

Greg sniffed.

Stanley produced a clean handkerchief and handed it to him.

Greg mopped himself up and mumbled thanks.

"Tell us what happened. We can't break the ties once and for all unless we understand exactly what you did."

Burke felt like a young mother coaxing her six-year-old to tell who started the fight after school. Years of living with Greg had honed her cajoling skills to a fine point, but it had been a while, thank God.

"I'm not some kind of loser," Greg told her.

She nodded encouragingly, but she had her fingers twisted together so tightly her knuckles were on the verge of snapping. "I know."

"You don't though. Not really," he sobbed.

Burke rolled her eyes. It would have been easier to get intel from a six-year-old kid.

"I'm not a loser. I'm an idiot, a complete and total idiot, a real dunce. The biggest dummy that ever walked on God's green earth."

"No one's arguing," Richard pointed out.

"I had everything," Greg said. "I was married to a gorgeous, successful woman. We had it made, didn't we, Babe? I mean the money, the house, we were so beautiful together. We could have had babies and puppies and lived the American dream, but I had to go and screw it all up."

Burke stood and turned her back on him.

"I'm sorry, Babe."

"Perhaps we should focus on the matter at hand," Stanley suggested.

"But I really am sorry," Greg whined.

Outside the window, snow began to fall again—everywhere except around the front door.

"It's far too little, way too late, Greg," Burke replied. "The woman you married is dead and gone. I think The Devil killed her in Tombstone. Or maybe it was the hidebehind in Colorado." She gazed at the ceiling like she might find the answer there. "Could have been the shadow demons."

Greg made a noise like a dog's squeaky toy. "Shadow demons?"

Burke faced him again, knowing she was about to lose the battle of keeping her temper under control. "Yes, Greg. Demons. I've seen more in the past year than most people see in a lifetime and that's good. It means I'm making a difference. I'm doing something with my life. I was never a good enough wife for you, but I'm a damn fine hunter, and because of that I'm going to save your sorry ass. In order to help me do that, you need to stop sniveling and tell us exactly what happened."

She happened to look at Richard's face just in time to see him blinking back tears. He grinned like she just won an Olympic gold medal. It was enough to melt the icy fury that held her in its grip, and she returned to her chair.

"Tell us what we're facing here." She barely kept from rolling her eyes. "And for the love of all that's holy, try your hardest to tell us the real and complete version, because if either of these men get murdered due to your lies, I will find you and I will peel your skin off with my silver blade, and I will burn your body while you're still alive."

All the blood drained from Greg's face. His Adam's apple bobbed, and he launched into his story, sharing everything Nathanial had already told them about and filling in the details. In all her life, Burke had never been especially prone to cursing, but she couldn't help but drop a few expletives.

"I don't know what you're so upset about," Greg said. "The Devil is gone, right? The priest is dead...again. The ghosts are gone. Annie Kay is...." He swallowed hard.

Richard stood and stomped over to the coffee pot. "You're about as bright as a box of rocks."

"Why don't you explain it to me, old man?" Greg snapped.

Burke ground her teeth.

"Greg, if I may." Stanley steepled his fingers under his chin. "I'd suggest that, first and foremost, you'd do well to be more polite to the man who saved your life, and very possibly your eternal soul, and nearly died in the process."

Greg's bottom lip poked out.

"Second, I remind you that you are the one who called us to help you. Here we are, helping, even though you misled us. If you feel like the job is done, no one is going to stop you from walking out that door and going on your merry way."

By the fireplace where he still stood, Gordon shifted, drawing Burke's attention. Given a million dollars, she wouldn't have been able to say what his thoughts were. The man could have made a fortune as a professional poker player, his face a mask of impassivity, though his eyes were alight with sharp intelligence. He had thoughts and ideas, but he wouldn't share them now. He was absorbing what he saw, to be processed later when he had time to think about it in peace.

Burke couldn't take her eyes off him. *Maybe if I knew him better, I could guess what he makes of all this. But I don't know him. He's practically a stranger.*

Stanley went on, and she focused on his words, telling herself there would be time to think about Gordon later. "Before you go, I ask you to ask yourself if you're really in any better position now than you were when you called us. Moonshadow Rising wants you dead, and whether or not her reasons for such extreme action are valid, they are no doubt a deeply held convictions of hers."

"I really don't know why she's so freaked out." Greg shook his head. "I mean, she can have the book back. It's not worth dying for. I don't want it anymore. I don't care if it really is full of powerful magic. I don't want it. It's too much."

Burke suddenly wondered why she ever thought he was stronger than her. That she needed him? All the weariness and worry of the past days settled on her shoulders, a physical ache that spread down her back and sank deep into her bones.

"I'm going to go take a shower and a nap. Stay. Go. I don't care." Her gaze drifted to Gordon, and he raised his brows. "We'll talk soon," she told him. "I'm just...I can't right now."

She made it all the way to the hall before Greg called out to her. "I heard it back there, Burke. You still love me."

With one hand braced against the doorframe she looked back over her shoulder. "Yes, I do. I figure I always will, but that doesn't mean I have to allow myself to be a part of your stupid little games. I helped you when you needed me."

"Now what?" he asked.

"Now I'm going to take a shower and a nap."

Stanley was sitting in the armchair in her room when Burke stepped out of the bathroom, hair and body wrapped in a towel.

"Wrong room, Stanley."

A fuzzy pink hoodie and some black leggings lay atop the pile next to her duffle. They'd do as well as anything.

"I was hoping to have a moment alone with you," he said.

She tugged the leggings up under her towel and pulled the hoodie over the top, pulled the knot loose and hung the towel over the arm of the chair. She stood there, waiting for him to say whatever he was going to say.

"How are you doing, my dear?"

I'm a hot mess. My body hurts in a hundred places because I'm the only one who didn't get any of Nathanial's magic lotion and my stomach is churning from the half-bottle of pain killers I've chugged down in the past few days. My ex-husband's life is still in danger and he's too stupid to care, and my boyfriend is hanging around in the background of my world waiting for me to give him some kind of signal and I can't even figure out if I want him here. What kind of stupid word is boyfriend anyway, for a man of his age?

She sat down to pull some fuzzy socks on. "I'm fine."

"You're the one who bathed me in cool water after The Devil locked me in the trunk of a car in the desert," Stanley said. "You've put your hand inside my body and literally touched my heart. You saw me at my weakest and lowest point."

Burke stared at the wooden planks beneath her feet.

"How are you doing, my dear?" he asked again.

"I'm confused and I'm tired."

Stanley rose, crossed the room, and kissed her head. "Rest. I have total faith in you."

He turned to leave.

"Stanley?" Burke wasn't ready for him to leave, but she didn't know what to say to him, either.

Stanley slipped his hands into the pockets of his neat gray

trousers and faced her. "In the course of a lifetime, our minds can grow immensely. We can gain wisdom beyond measure, but our hearts remain foolish as long as they beat."

She wondered if she'd be as wise as Stanley if she lived another hundred years.

A knock sounded on the door and Stanley opened it.

Gordon stood there, strong and handsome and so still it bordered on preternatural. "Sorry. Am I interrupting?"

"Not at all. I was just headed out," Stanley said.

The two men passed each other. When Gordon gently pushed the door shut, then faced her, she stood. "Thinking about you has driven me to distraction these past few weeks," he said. "Now I'm wondering if it was all just a fantasy. Did I drive across the country just to see the sights?"

Greg almost died because he brushed against the supernatural. What would happen to Gordon? What would happen to her grandfather and Stanley if she allowed herself to be distracted? What would happen to them if Gordon left her, and she fell apart the way she had when Greg had left her? Breathing hurt. She knew what she had to do.

"Maybe. I was wrong. I shouldn't have invited you to come with us," she said.

"Do you want me here?" Gordon asked.

She swallowed the painful lump in her throat. "Not really. I'm sorry. It was a mistake."

Gordon stepped closer. "Don't lie to me."

"I'm not lying to you."

His eyes were dark as onyx, his voice a low rumble in her belly. "Then you're lying to yourself." He stood so close, the warmth from his body lit a coal in her center.

"You don't know me." She had to choke the words out.

"Let me know you, Burke." He pressed her against the wall with his whole body.

Her core turned to molten lava. "Gordon, don't do this."

His lips brushed against her neck. He nipped at her ear.

"Gordon, no!" She hadn't meant to shout, but there it was.

His body sagged against her for a moment, then he straightened and took a step back. "Okay."

What was molten a moment earlier turned hard and cold. "Okay?"

"I'll go if that's what you want. I have never forced myself on a woman in any way. I'm not going to start today, but I'm sorry as hell that it turned out this way. We could have...well...anyway." He strode to the door.

Burke stayed with her back against the wall, afraid that if she moved her legs would fail her. She watched his hand reach for the knob, watched the door swing open on its old brass hinges.

"See ya around, Burke Martin. Watch out for monsters, will you?" he said, his back to her.

She watched him leave and stood there alone, frozen, panicked.

What have I done?

It's a wise woman who moves through life with caution and awareness, Stanley had said. *But there's a fine line between caution and fear. Nothing good has ever come to anyone who was ruled by their fear. Everything worth having lies on the other side of fear.*

Burke had faced death more often in the past year than most people could even conceive. Twice, now, she'd confronted The Devil Herself. She'd nearly lost all three of the people she most loved. None of that was as scary as her feelings for Gordon. The emotion was too much, too big, too volatile. Giving in would mean giving herself—her whole self—into his power. He'd be able to wound her more deeply than Greg ever had, and Greg left her floundering for years.

This is different.

Gordon is different.

What if he isn't?

I'm different.

And that was the real crux, wasn't it? She married Greg as a way to make herself feel whole and complete. She didn't need Gordon to complete her. She was her own person now, strong and capable and sure of her place in the world.

But she wanted him.

Oh, dear God, I want him.

The spell broke and her legs were freed. She ran to the door and yanked it open, intending to chase him down the hall and out to the driveway, praying she wasn't too late, and she almost couldn't stop fast enough to avoid colliding with him.

"Burke!" he cried.

They faced each other, both of them panting with surprise and adrenaline.

"You're still here," she said.

"I was trying to work up to one more sales pitch."

She couldn't help but smile. "I'm sold, Gordon."

His lips crashed down on hers, and his strong arms were around her, and the scent of his subtle cologne turned her brain deliciously fuzzy. When he steered her back into the room and kicked the door shut, she couldn't even remember why she'd been so scared in the first place.

CHAPTER TWENTY-THREE

Richard

STANLEY SAID THERE WAS NO GOOD WAY TO TRACK THE WITCH. A tracking spell required something that belonged to her and the only thing they had was the book. Trying to weave magic over an object so powerful was an invitation to disaster, and so they were at loose ends.

"So, what? We book another cruise and go put our feet up?" Richard asked.

He paced back and forth in front of the window while the rest of them sat around the table and the fireplace. Feeling great had a downside. All that pent-up energy left him restless as a tiger in a cage.

"I think we should return to Villa Cierto," Stanley said.

Richard halted. "You lost your dang marbles? The haunted nursing home? I always knew you were two cards short of a deck, but this is your most bone-headed idea so far."

"I think he's right," Burke said.

Richard harrumphed. How could he trust the kid's judgement? She came skipping out of her room with stars in her eyes, trying to act like nothing was up when they all knew darn well Gordon's boots had been under her bed all night long. In his experience, young people in the throes of the honeymoon phase of a relationship had as much good sense as a deer on the highway.

"Don't snort at me," she said.

Richard scowled.

"It's a good idea. Kenneth knows what's up around here, and when we were wandering around without a clue before, that's where the action started."

"That action was us, dang near getting killed, and The Devil showing up to stick her meddling head into our business," Richard said.

When Stanley spoke, his voice was so quiet Richard could barely make out the words. "Christine is there, too."

"Christine who?"

"The doctor," Stanley said. "Christine. She...." He left that hanging there like a half-woven spider's web.

A fuzzy memory of a pretty young lady doctor drifted through Richard's mind. Somewhere in the helter-skelter mess of the past few days, the bizarre interaction between Stan Kapcheck and the girl who clearly knew him from some past hunt had faded away to just about nothing.

"What's she got to do with this?" he asked.

Stanley shrugged. "Nothing, so far as I know, but I have unfinished business with her. Since we've no better ideas, we may as well kill two birds with one stone."

"Sounds good. It's time to wrap this up and move on," Burke said.

Still convinced it was a bad idea, Richard found himself nevertheless riding shotgun as Stanley navigated the Cadillac carefully along the icy roads to town. Burke sat in the backseat looking like the world's most uncomfortable sardine. To her left, her current lover tried hard to give the appearance of stoicism, but he couldn't seem to help himself from growing twinkly-eyed and loopy from time to time. To her right, the idiot pouted like a kid who got sent to the corner.

Villa Cierto's parking lot had been plowed and now sported a ring of grimy gray snow piles around the edges. The five of them piled out of the car like clowns under the big top and trouped inside. Neither the receptionist's helmet hair nor her horrid blue eyeshadow had changed. Richard thought she might have even been wearing the same ugly sweater as last time.

Stanley laid it on thick as pea soup. "The cool air agrees with you. You're absolutely glowing this morning."

"Ain't never met an FBI agent that resorted to flattery. Ain't never met one who dragged half a bus-load of folks with him wherever he went, either," she said.

"You're as astute as you are lovely." Stan Kapcheck had a gift for using lots of words but not saying much at all. "We'd like to speak with Kenneth, please."

"Kenneth left and he hasn't come back. My best guess is that he headed back to the pueblo. If you were real FBI, that would be bad news, since you wouldn't have jurisdiction there."

Burke leaned one shoulder against the wall. "Have you really had so many encounters with the FBI?"

The woman narrowed her painted eyes. "Don't presume to know me."

"I wouldn't dare," Burke assured the ornery old bat.

"May we speak with the doctor, then?" Stanley asked.

"The doctor's busy."

"It's very important," Burke said.

She pinned him with a stare. "You got a warrant?"

Stanley held up his hands in a gesture of surrender. "We just have a few questions."

"And the doctor's got a few people dying back there who need her more than you do. Come back when you've got enough due cause to convince a judge to order the doc to talk." Her gaze landed on Gordon. "Now, you, I could actually believe as FBI. They should have you be the front-man from now on."

"I appreciate the vote of confidence," Gordon said. "But you've got it all wrong. I'm the dead weight in this group."

The receptionist snorted and pulled the frosted glass window shut without further comment.

"Get a warmer reception from a rabid porcupine," Richard observed.

"I can still hear you," the woman said.

Richard stuck his tongue out at the glass knowing full well she couldn't see him do it.

Stanley patted him on the back and retreated out the door, but then drew to a halt so fast, the rest of them did a fine imitation of a bunch of stooges crashing into one another. The lady doctor stood still as death at the edge of the parking lot, her arms limp at her sides.

Stanley disentangled himself from the pileup and crept up beside her as cautiously as a person would approach a frightened baby lion. "Christine?"

"His car." She gave a barely perceptible nod in the direction of the Cadillac.

Stanley nodded. "Yeah."

"It's exactly like I remember." She inched toward the car.

Stanley stayed at her side and, at last, they arrived at the curb. She stepped down and brushed her fingertips along the convertible's cloth top.

"He loved this car."

"It was the only possession he ever cared about," Stanley agreed.

She peered up at him with wide eyes. "So, he really is dead, then? He wouldn't have given you this otherwise."

Stanley took a breath that puffed up his skinny chest and when he let it out, for just a second, he looked the sad, frightened weakling he'd been after all the stuff that had happened with The

Children of Cain. Then he gathered his composure around himself like a finely tailored suit.

"The Busar I knew for so very, very long is dead," he replied. "He's been destroyed by wounds that no man can recover from, and yet...."

"He's still alive," she said.

"Yes. I believe he is."

Burke and Richard exchanged a glance. Did Stanley just say that his mentor was still alive? He'd been telling them for a year the man was dead. Richard scratched his head. Had he, though? Had he ever actually said the man was dead?

Gone.

Repeatedly, Stanley told them Busar was gone. He'd left it up to them to interpret that and he'd refused to tell them what happened.

A gust of wind swept down from the mountaintop, carrying the scent of snow. The doctor pulled the collar of her thin lab coat tight as if that would offer some real protection from the elements.

She hunched her shoulders. "If he's still out there you have to stop him."

Stanley drooped like a houseplant in the shade. "Christine, I can't...."

"That's a load of bull, and you know it," she snapped.

Richard opened his mouth to defend Stanley, but Burke grabbed his forearm and he understood that she was trying to tell him it wasn't their conversation. Whatever past Stanley shared with the lady doctor it was between the two of them and he had no part in it.

"The things I saw, what happened to me when I was a kid...." She pressed a hand against the hood of the car as if drawing strength from it. "Back then, Busar told me that he lived the way he did because someone had to stand in the gap between humankind and real evil and, if not him, then who?"

Stanley rocked on the toes of his shiny wingtips. "That sounds like Busar."

"But now he's not standing in the gap."

Based on Stanley's stony expression, Richard wasn't sure if the man was getting ready to answer or knock her lights out.

Finally, Stanley said, "Busar no longer stands in the gap."

"Then it's up to you," she said.

"Is that not what I've done here in Santa Fe? I've given more of myself than you know, to do what must be done."

She shook her head. "Maybe you've done good in your way, but if he's out there and you've let him be, all you've done is run away."

"He's like a father to me. Could you kill your father?" he whispered.

Her eyes narrowed. "You know what I've done and why."

"That wasn't you," Stanley said.

"Then why can I still, to this day, remember what it felt like when that knife sliced through their flesh?" She took a deep breath. "If you claim the title of hunter, go hunt, Stanley Kapcheck. Stop running away." She stalked back into the nursing home, and they all watched her go.

Burke was the first to move. She laid a gentle hand on Stanley's shoulder.

He shrugged it off. "We need to find the witch."

"The witch found you."

They all jumped at the sound of Moonshadow Riding's voice. She stood in the scrawny shadow of the nearest mesquite tree. Sunlight glinted off the silver gun in her right hand.

"Enough with games and magic. All I wanted was Greg, dead. Let's do this the simple way." She lifted the gun and the entire group scrambled.

Gordon shoved Greg behind him. Burke and Richard drew their own weapons, and Stanley spread his arms wide as if he had the power to shield them all through sheer force of will.

"Will you shoot us all, my dear?" Stanley asked.

She kept the gun trained on Greg. "If I have to."

"You'll be dead four times over before you hit the ground," Burke said.

The witch gave a twitchy little shrug. "I suppose that will be justice. At least justice will be served to him, too."

"I wasn't even with you, you crazy bitch," Greg whined from where he cowered behind Gordon.

"You were with me, Greg. You left me for her, and I was willing to accept that because I thought maybe you'd make her happy. That's not how it worked out, was it? I was a fool, but I'm not a fool anymore. I will kill the man who killed my sister, and if I die too, then so be it." She took a breath and steadied her aim.

"You're crazy. I never killed anybody," he cried. "She threw me out, so I left."

If looks could kill, the idiot would already be dead. Richard wouldn't have been surprised to see flames shoot out of the woman's eyes. Her rage was a tangible presence.

"Yes, Greg. You left. You left and you stole what she'd bound to herself for safe keeping, and then when she tried to get it back, you used it against her."

Stanley lowered his arms. "She bound the book of necromancy with blood magic?"

Moonshadow Rising answered through gritted teeth. "That's right. She didn't want it to fall into the wrong hands."

"He didn't know," Stanley said.

"He knew enough to draw a soul out of Hell," she shot back. "When he cast that spell, my sister died. A life, for a life. He murdered her as sure as if he shot her in the head, which is what I'm going to do to him."

Greg peeked out from behind his guard. "Running Brook is dead?"

The witch's entire body trembled in the grip of her anger.

"He was ignorant," Burke said.

"That doesn't excuse his actions. He was pretty and cowardly and selfish, and his actions stole my sister."

"Blood doesn't pay for blood," Stanley said.

"Then what does?"

"Forgiveness."

She took her eyes off Greg long enough to study Stanley's face. "Would you forgive, if it was someone you loved?"

The two of them stared at each other so long Richard's arms began to tremble from the strain of holding his gun out in front of himself. He'd have bet his bippy the witch was going to take her shot. Things were about to turn into a regular OK Corral. How many shots could she fire before he and Burke took her down? There was no more healing balm. Stanley would take the first bullet. He was in front. The second would hit either Gordon or Burke. Odds were solid that when it was all said and done, their idiot ex who started all this would be the only one left standing.

No way was that going to happen on Richard's watch.

Resolve flooded his muscles, steadying his trembling arms. He sighted down the short barrel of his gun carefully and, just as Stanley had taught him, he inhaled, preparing to squeeze the trigger with his exhale.

Bang!

Richard nearly jumped out of his skin.

The witch gasped and fell to the ground.

What happened?

He looked over at Burke who still had her weapon pointed at the other woman. She ran forward and kicked the silver gun away. Blood pooled around the witch's thigh in exactly the spot Richard had aimed. It shouldn't have been any more than a flesh wound, but even as he watched the girl twitched and began to give up the fight.

Tears pooled in her eyes. "It's not fair."

Stanley squatted down next to her. "It never is."

Moonshadow Rising lay her head down on the snowy sidewalk outside of the haunted nursing home and died while three hunters and the two men who loved Burke bore witness.

Greg sniffled like a little kid.

"I don't get it," Gordon muttered.

Burke held up her gun. "The bullets are dipped in holy water. She'd given herself over to black magic. It wasn't the gunshot that killed her."

"More like an allergic reaction," Stanley said.

"Why'd you shoot her?" Greg asked in a squeaky voice.

Burke holstered her weapon. "She would have killed us all to get to you. We would have fired back. Everybody but you would be dead. You're not worth that level of sacrifice." She pulled her phone from her pocket and dialed, presumably to feed some story to the cops.

Richard had to hand it to her. She was good at exit lines.

CHAPTER TWENTY-FOUR

Greg

TWO DIVORCES AND A YEAR OF ROAMING HAD WHITTLED
Greg's possessions down to a few bags that fit neatly in the trunk
of his car. He stared at the meager collection and found himself in
the grip of sadness and regret. He had a good thing when he was
married to Burke, and he blew it by cheating on her. He had a
good thing with his second wife, and he blew it again. The closest
he'd ever come to a healthy relationship was when he'd been with
the dead woman who ate people.

He had a head for business, but his messy relationships ruined
any opportunity he might have had to climb the corporate ladder.
He couldn't even make a success of living in a hippie commune
where people spent their days smoking pot and weaving baskets.
What purpose did his life have? What did it all mean? He'd seen
The Devil and touched real magic and now he was right back in
this same old place. Alone. Nowhere to go. Nothing to do.

Did it have to be that way?

Burke floundered after the divorce. He'd seen it and felt guilty
about it. She'd been so successful and then she just faded from life

after they broke up. But then something happened to her. She was more beautiful in her forties than her twenty-something self ever could have dreamed of being. And she was so damn strong, physically, mentally, emotionally. What gave a person that kind of fortitude? What happened in the past year?

She started hunting with Stanley and Richard.

She was like some kind of superhero in pink sweatpants.

He slammed the lid of the trunk shut, and there she stood in the snow, watching him.

"Where will you go?" she asked.

"I need to get a life." It was the most truthful thing he could think to say, and she didn't argue. "It could have been good for us."

"Yes, it could have," Burke agreed.

"Will you marry Gordon?"

She glanced over her shoulder as if to see if Gordon was listening in. "We haven't gotten that far."

"I let my fear and my desire, my weakness, get in the way of us. I'm sorry for that." He reached for the door handle. Over the course of years, he'd gotten good at running away and he was ready to make his escape now. "Thank you, for everything."

"It's what we do," she said. "So where will you go?"

Again and again, he'd pushed the thought aside, but it popped out of his mouth despite his best efforts. "Maybe I could be a hunter, too."

Her laughter bruised his pride. "That is a terrible idea, Greg. You'll be dead in a week."

His hand fell away from the door handle. "You lived."

"You're not me."

"You think you're better than me?" he asked.

"I think you lack focus. You can't let your guard down for a second in this job. If you do, you die." Her gaze drifted toward the horizon. "Or worse."

"Do you ever make mistakes?"

She wrapped her arms around herself. "You should go. Get a place somewhere warm and green. Start a little business. Maybe go into real estate. You'd be good at that. You've always had a great mind for business."

Funny how she always knew his thoughts. "You said you loved me."

"I loved you then, and I love you now, but somewhere along the line I came to realize that love is a choice. That one choice alone isn't nearly strong enough to be the foundation for a relationship."

"What do you need, then? What does the old cop have that I don't?" He hoped the question didn't sound as needy as he felt.

Long, slow breaths that came before speaking seemed to be a habit she'd cultivated since they'd split up. "He has my trust. He has my respect."

"Is that enough?"

At last, she looked at him, but didn't answer his question. "Drive safe," she said, and then she left him alone.

Greg slid into the driver's seat and started the engine. All of North America lay open before him, but where to go? He'd overheard Stanley make a comment about hunters being led to their hunts. Maybe that could be true for him, too. He was no hunter, Burke was right about that, but maybe whatever led them from one adventure to the next could lead him as well. He pressed the gas and began the long descent out of the Sangre De Cristo Mountains.

CHAPTER TWENTY-FIVE

Richard

IN EIGHT DECADES, RICHARD HAD NEVER KNOWN ANYONE WHO talked more than Stanley Kapcheck—a fact that made his current silence entirely disturbing. The old peacock looked just as preened and prissy as ever in gray slacks and a red waistcoat with the little gold chain. But he sat in front of the fire and stared at the flames like he was trying to read the future there. Heck, maybe he was. That wouldn't be the strangest thing Richard had seen someone do in the past year, not by a long shot.

When pressed, Stanley just said he was "musing, as old men are prone to do." It was Burke who finally plopped down in a chair and demanded he talk.

"Something's up, and we deserve to know what it is," she said. "Tell us about Busar and tell us where the next hunt is because it's pretty obvious to anyone with eyes that you're the one being led now."

Behind them, at the kitchen table, Gordon and Nathanial grew quiet over the chessboard they'd set up between them.

For a long time, Richard had struggled to figure out why it was so blasted difficult to make out what Stanley was thinking. Finally, it dawned on him that it was his eyes. He had a twinkle in his eye that reminded Richard of the old Dennis the Menace television show, and little creases around the corners of his eyes that made him look like he was constantly on the verge of laughter, even when he was sad or angry or hurt.

"You're right. You do deserve to know," Stanley said. Then he went back to staring at the fire like it held the secrets of the universe.

Richard harrumphed. "That ain't no kind of an answer, man."

Nathanial moved his chess piece and spoke up. "There are some things that are best not spoken aloud. Giving them voice brings them to life. Others, fall to dust upon being mentioned. Know your nemesis, Stanley, and consider which type it is."

A tear spilled from the corner of Stanley's eye, and he made no effort to wipe it away or hide it.

Burke slid out of her chair and knelt at his feet like a disciple. She took his wrinkled old hand between both of hers. "We owe you our lives, Stanley. Tell us."

He nodded and pursed his lips as if considering how to begin. "I told you how I became a hunter. When I was a boy, a totem fell into my hands and changed who I was. Busar was there. He helped me, saved me, molded me into the man I am today. It was Busar who tracked the skinwalker that brought us all together. The car is Busar's. The cash we spend came from Busar's family fortune. I owe him everything, and I do mean everything. I'd have lost not only my life but my very soul several times over if not for the man who was more of a father to me than anyone who contributed to the genetic makeup of my body."

The conversation from the nursing home parking lot came back to Richard. Lately, he'd had a lot of thoughts about things that were worse than death. "When you said he was gone, you meant the man as you knew him."

Stanley gave a slow nod. "He fought a terrible evil, a true

abomination. It would have killed Christine. It could have decimated cities."

"Nobody wins every fight," Burke said.

Stanley pulled his hand away from hers and rubbed his chin. "Busar won. He won every fight. He saved Christine and countless others."

If a pin hit the floor, it would have sounded like thunder in the silence while they all waited for him to tell them the rest.

"He ripped his soul," Stanley said.

Nathanial made a sound that would have been better suited to the surly cat.

"What does that mean?" Richard demanded.

"It means he's not a human, nor is he a monster. Such a thing has no business existing at all. He can't die, and he can't live. He can only destroy everything he touches."

Burke sat back on her heels. "We'd have heard if something so horrible was out there."

"I have heard," Stanley replied. "I know where he is. I know what he's done."

Nathanial's voice carried a palpable weight of sadness. "You have to go, Stanley."

"I know." His watery eyes settled on Burke and then Richard. "I have to go, and I have to go alone."

Burke shot to her feet. "No."

The legs of the wooden chair screeched against the stone floor when Gordon rose. He came to stand behind Burke and pulled her back against him.

"It's not your hunt," Stanley said.

"We're supposed to say our goodbyes and send you after him on your own?" Burke asked. She didn't fight Gordon's hold on her, but acid dripped from her words.

"It's my mess to clean up. I ran away from my responsibility. I let an evil fester this long. Now it's come back to me, and I need to attend to what I've neglected." Stanley stood and wiped his eyes. "I'll leave as soon as I get my things packed."

Richard heaved himself up out of the big chair, uncertain that he had the right words to express what he was thinking, but very sure something needed to be said. "You're about as thick as a brick if you think me and the kid are going to say goodbye and send you off to fight whatever this thing is on your own after all you've done for us."

Stanley's shoulders sagged. "Dick, I can't—"

"Bull hockey!" Richard balled his hands into fists and scowled at the only real friend he'd had since he was little more than a boy. "If you go, we'll follow you. We'll find you. We'll figure out how to kill him before you even get there."

"He'll kill you first," Stanley said. "Or worse."

"Then it'll be on you, because you're the one who split this team up." He wagged a wrinkled old finger in Stanley's face. "And before you give me some kind of load of dung about this being your hunt, the strigoi came to me and you helped. The skinwalker was ours, and Burke saved our old hides. That little geek in Michigan was Burke's. Should we have let him kill her? And The Devil—"

What about The Devil? Where had she gone, anyway? And if she had a way of getting back to them, what were they in for then? Those were questions for another day.

"We're a team," Richard finished, somewhat lamely.

Those little wrinkles at the corners of Stanley's eyes scrunched up. "All right, then, but don't say I didn't warn you." He looked at Gordon. "You're out of the frying pan and into the fire if you come with us."

"I damn near died of boredom, floating around the Caribbean filling out reports about petty theft. If I go down with a gun in my hand, I call that a win," Gordon said.

Richard couldn't remember the last time he related so deeply to anything. He turned to see Nathanial sitting at the table, shaking and pale as a sheet.

"What's the matter with you?" Richard demanded.

Nathanial wrapped the end of his long beard around one meaty fist. "Only the Hand of God can help you if you go."

Stanley slapped him on the shoulder as he walked past on his way to his room. "So be it."

Richard hadn't the foggiest clue what that meant, but for some reason a little spark of excitement pushed back the darkness of his fear and he had a spring in his step when he headed off to gather his own belongings. Whatever came next, Gordon was right. It wouldn't be boring.

SOME FRIENDSHIPS NEVER DIE

Solve mystery.
Save children.
Face past.

Richard, Stanley, and Burke have hunted monsters of every ilk, but what can they do when fate points them toward a creature that cannot be killed—a creature that was once Stanley's dearest friend and whom he abandoned thirty years earlier?

Children are dying, the medical examiner is a monster, there's a mischievous witch in town, and Stanley's old girlfriend is still carrying a flame for him. Revealing the secrets of the past is about to lead the hunters toward a future they never saw coming.

CHAPTER ONE

Richard

THE FIRE-ENGINE-RED 1959 CADILLAC COUPE DEVILLE streaked across the jagged spine of the Rocky Mountains. On the vehicle's fine stereo, Elvis Presley sang about hound dogs. Bright winter sun beat down through the windshield, warming Richard Bell. In such grand moments, he could almost forget that the world was infested with blood-thirsty monsters. Each mile brought him and his companions closer to their next encounter, but at this moment, all was right with the world.

He took a bite of the burger he'd ordered from a roadside stand. Ketchup and bacon grease dripped down his chin. He closed his eyes and relished the savory mix of meat, onions, veggies, and cheese. In all his years of retirement and his brief stay at the old folks' home, he'd eaten only to stay alive. What a mistake! Eating wasn't a means to an end. Good food was, all by itself, a reason for living.

A salty french fry was the perfect complement to the burger. He washed the food down with icy cold soda and was rewarded with a satisfying belch.

No one reproached him. *Weird.*

He peeked over his shoulder into the backseat. His grand-daughter—a woman old enough to have grandkids of her own, had she started at an early age—was canoodling with her new man-friend, Gordon Westchester. The two looked like teenagers, whispering and giggling with their heads together. They'd been that way since they left Santa Fe a day and a half earlier.

Stanley Kapcheck sat in the driver's seat, dapper in his zippered sweater and blue jeans. He wore a pair of over-priced sunglasses and a newsboy cap that covered his shiny bald head. Richard thought he looked like a wrinkled old raisin striving too hard for a younger man's style, but judging by the way both women and men threw themselves at the geezer, he was doing something right. Richard gave a mental shrug. He'd rather be comfortable in his Hanes t-shirts. Besides, trading in the perfectly serviceable Wellington Plastics jacket he'd been wearing for the last twenty years seemed wasteful. Nothing wrong with it. Why buy new?

"You're pretty quiet," Richard said before taking another bite of the divine hamburger.

Stanley's thin lips twitched in a semblance of a smile, and he replied in his impeccable British accent, "I suppose the dialogue in my mind occupies me to the point of distraction."

"Voices in your head, eh? Always knew there was something wrong with you."

"Don't you converse with yourself in your thoughts?"

"I ain't crazy." Richard refused to get drawn into Stanley's nonsense. Talking to voices inside your own head—that's the kind of thing that got a man locked up in a padded room.

"My friend, we are old men chasing after death in an old car, armed with swords and wooden stakes. We're both certifiably insane."

Richard harrumphed. "You ain't got to say it that way. We're doing a service for this world."

"Yes. I suppose we are."

From the back seat, Burke chimed in. "Grandpa's right and Busar was doing a service, too. How many lives did he save? How many have you saved because of what he taught you?"

Stanley down-shifted as they began a long, curving descent.

"Then you taught us, me and Burke, and now Gordon," Richard said. "We ain't even been doing this for a whole year yet, and we helped a heap of folks. It's good work, and it all started with Busar."

"It all started thousands of years before Busar was born," Stanley replied. "He had a mentor, too, of course, just as he mentored me." With skillful ease, born from having driven thousands upon thousands of miles in his lifetime, Stanley maneuvered the car along a narrow stretch bordered by a solid rock wall on one side and a two-hundred-foot drop on the other. "Busar, as I knew him, is dead. My mentor was murdered in a horrible accident while we were hunting a monster that preyed on children. An honorable way to go, and that's how I prefer to think of it."

Richard scratched his head. He tried to pat down his white cloud of hair, realized he failed, and wondered why, after so many years, he kept trying. An idea had nagged him since they left for this hunt, and he hadn't had the backbone to spit it out. It was now or never.

"We saved you, Stanley. Burke, too."

Nothing about Stanley's expression changed. As usual, he remained cool as a cucumber.

Richard wanted to ignore him but couldn't.

How annoying. It ain't natural.

Tension buzzed in the car like a fat, bloodthirsty mosquito.

In an attempt to swat it away, Richard barreled on with his theory. In for a penny, in for a pound. "You told us that Busar was fighting the monster, and his soul ripped, but you ripped too. Back when we fought on the beach in Michigan, they ripped part of you away, and that leprechaun fixed you up again."

He took a sip of his soda to wash away the absurdity of that sentence. Talk about sending a guy to the loony bin! A year ago, he'd have thought such a comment the height of insanity, but he'd had his eyes opened since then.

"Burke got split up, too."

A rustling of fabric from the back seat, then Burke appeared, leaning over the back of the seat. "I was never split. I was possessed."

"What's the difference?" Richard hated nitpicking.

"If something's split, it's only half. I was double. Still, I think you have a valid point. I've been wondering the same thing. There are all kinds of cures for—"

"There is no cure." Stanley's flat tone left no room for argument, but he'd softened back to his usual over-dandied style when he spoke again. "Forgive me, my dear. I don't mean to be churlish, but my spirit is weary, and I cannot bear the discussion of miracles when the likelihood is so slim."

Burke squeezed Stanley's arm and scooted back next to Gordon again.

"Okay, so I'm the new guy," Gordon growled, his voice like crushed lava stone. "I've seen enough that I get the general idea. I met the sea god and fought a monster on the cruise ship. I saw what happened back there in Santa Fe when Burke's ex played with magic. Consider my mind opened. But I'd like a little more in-depth explanation of what we're heading into here. What are you thinking we're going to do when we get there?"

The same questions occurred to Richard repeatedly, but he'd been too big of a chicken to put them out there like that. He wasn't entirely sure he wanted to know the answers. Sometimes ignorance was bliss.

White wall tires hummed a tenor melody over the V8 engine's bass growl. The three less-experienced hunters waited for Stanley to teach them something new.

"Certain creatures cross cultural boundaries," he began.

"Every culture, no matter how primitive or modern, share the ancient stories of demons, blood drinkers, vengeful spirits, and so on and so forth. The monsters of the legends that spread across the globe are the most ancient and most powerful."

Richard still had a third of a cheeseburger lying on a wrapper on his lap. Cooler now, it was a bit past its peak, but still infinitely better than the olive loaf sandwiches he'd lived off of for half a century before Stanley sprung him out of the old folk's home.

Stanley slowed behind a semi, peeked around at the oncoming traffic, and passed as smooth as a seasoned racecar driver. "Busar was killed fighting an entity so old its name has been lost to antiquity."

Once again, the urge to point out that Busar wasn't dead rose up in Richard like a burp, but he managed to force the impulse back down. He would have said it a year ago. He was growing as a person.

"So, you're saying that the old things are the worst, and this one is the oldest of all?" Gordon asked.

"Not the oldest of all, I should think, but old beyond human memory. For lack of a better term, we're about to pick a fight with the boogeyman," Richard said.

Now that the burger was gone, Richard wondered if the entire meal might have been poor judgment. It sat in his gut like a brick. He took another drink of soda, hoping to work himself up to a proper belch to relieve the pressure. Admitting that it was fear churning in his protruding belly was out of the question. Almost certainly, it was the greasy food.

"My mama told me the boogeyman was a figment of my imagination," Gordon said.

Stanley's gaze never left the road. "Your mother also told you all souls went to Heaven. She was mistaken."

Once again, Burke's head popped up between them. Kid used to be some kind of a hippie-dippie yoga master, always breathing deep and finding her Zen. Give her a few days with a deep-voiced ex-soldier and all of a sudden, she's restless as a worm in hot ashes.

"You've been talking around the edges of this hunt since the subject of Busar came up back in Santa Fe. Spell it out. What are we heading into? Let's make a plan. It'll be better for you than letting your thoughts eat you from the inside out," she said.

They reached a more level stretch of pavement, and Stanley adjusted the gearshift. "Your wisdom exceeds your years."

"I have plenty of years," Burke said.

Gordon whispered something Richard couldn't make out, and Burke flashed a grin in his direction.

Good Lord. Maybe his indigestion wasn't caused by the food after all. Still, the kid had a point. "We got nothing but time. There's what? Another six hundred miles between here and there?"

Stanley's nod was so subtle it might have been a twitch of his old muscles if only Stanley's old muscles ever twitched. No man who remembered the Roaring Twenties had a right to be steady as steel. Time is a transaction. For every day living, a body has to give up a piece of itself. So far as he could tell, the only thing Stan Kapcheck ever had to give up was his hair.

"Are you okay?" Burke asked.

Richard twisted around to look at her. "Me? I'm fine. Why?"

"You had a look on your face like you just ate a sour pickle. You're not car sick, are you? These twisty roads—"

"I'm fine," Richard groused. "Can we stick to the subject, please? Spill it, Stan. You've got to do it sooner or later."

"I'll begin with the monster, and perhaps that will help you understand about Busar. As I said, we're fighting the boogeyman. It's an entity that, like a ghost, can be there one moment and gone the next, but trapping it is far more difficult than trapping a ghost or even a demon. No mere salt line or devil's trap will hold it."

"But it can be trapped?" Burke asked.

"It can, but it's powerful magic that requires tools beyond what we have."

"A hunter is led to the hunt. The tools tend to be there when we need them." Burke was parroting something Stanley had repeated a thousand times.

"Yes, but...." Stanley let that argument drift away and started on a different track. "Children have an uncanny sense of this creature's presence. It terrifies them, and it feeds on their terror. It will play with them, sometimes for months, even years, before it destroys them. The deaths themselves will seem so natural no one ever thinks to question. A little one will develop a fever, they'll be lethargic. The child's condition deteriorates from that point."

"It could be the flu, so far as everyone around them is concerned," Burke observed.

"And so hunters rarely become aware," Stanley added.

Gordon piped up from the back seat. "Even if they're aware, what can they do against something that can't be killed and is nearly impossible to trap?"

"You've come to the crux of the problem," Stanley said.

Richard remembered something that had been mentioned when all this first came up. "You told us before that Busar had a talisman he was using."

"He did."

"Can we get something like that again?"

"Something like a magical seven-thousand-year-old artifact?" Stanley shrugged a bony shoulder. "So far as I know, the one we had was the only one that existed, but I'm open to suggestions if you know where such a thing might be found."

"You have connections," Richard pointed out.

"Having connections doesn't make the acquisition of such objects as simple as popping into the local Piggly Wiggly, Dick."

Richard harrumphed. Lord, but he hated being called Dick, and Stan Kapcheck darn well knew it.

"Even if we had such an object," Stanley went on, "the risk is too high. I won't watch what happened to Busar happen to any of you. I won't make this journey a second time."

"Maybe The Children of Cain could help us," Burke suggested.

Now *that* was a humdinger of an idea. No one had more powerful objects than the super-secret organization that governed the world's monsters.

"My dear, don't forget that The Children of Cain are on the side of the monsters, not the humans. The only reason they helped us in the past is because it suited their needs. I will remind you, as well, that a part of their kindness toward us had to do with The Devil's hands-off order. I suspect after recent events she may not be so inclined to offer me her protection."

Oh, yeah. The Devil probably wanted to kill them. That was a problem. Richard opened the glovebox and fished out a bottle of antacids.

"Do I want to know who The Children of Cain are?" Gordon asked.

"No," the three said in unison.

"Is this boogeyman mentioned in the books of lore?" Burke asked.

"Of course," Stanley said.

"You going to tell us what it says, or are we playing twenty questions to pass the time?" Richard asked.

"The lore says the creatures are to be avoided at all costs." Stanley's plumb line posture drooped a little. "You're all failing to see the main point." He sighed and sat up straight again as if steeling himself. "The creature Busar and I fought died when Busar did."

Richard opened his mouth to argue about Busar being dead, but Stanley held up a hand to silence him.

"Children were dying. When Busar.... When all that happened, the deaths stopped. I don't know where Busar went, but the deaths stopped, and the child we were helping thrived and grew up. I kept tabs on her and on the area all this time. I don't know where Busar went, but the deaths stopped."

"And now it's started again," Burke said.

Stanley nodded. "Yes. Two children have passed away in the last year, both from a mysterious, undiagnosed illness, but the monster is dead. The odds of another coming to the same place are hard to put stock in. Boogymen are fiercely territorial, and only a few of the creatures exist."

The edge of the setting sun dipped behind the mountain, casting the landscape into sudden twilight. Stanley removed his sunglasses and stowed them in the center console.

He met Burke's gaze in the rearview mirror. "I told you before. A human with half a soul is neither in this world nor the next. He cannot live, cannot experience pleasure, cannot love, cannot exist among whole humans without causing constant violent disruption to the balance of their lives, whether that's what he desires or not. Nor can he die, as a significant piece of him is already crossed over. He is trapped in his existence, living in an unending battle of what he was and cannot become."

"I can't quite wrap my mind around what you're telling us," Gordon growled. "I get the idea, but I guess I haven't seen enough of this kind of thing to accept it the way you all do. That said, maybe my question is ignorant. If that's the case, I thank you for helping me get up to speed. If Busar successfully eliminated the monster and you say another of the same kind is unlikely to hunt in the same area, then we're not hunting this so-called boogeyman. And you said yourself that you've kept an eye on the area. If Busar had turned serial killer or some such thing, you'd have known long before now. It's not Busar hurting these children. He doesn't have the power to drain them like the other creature does."

"Maybe they're just getting sick," Burke suggested.

"Maybe Busar started walking north and ended up hunting whales in the arctic sea," Richard said.

"Maybe there's a different monster causing this trouble. Are there other monsters on the Olympic Peninsula?" Gordon asked.

"My friend, there are so many monsters on the Olympic Peninsula. Our first challenge will be figuring out who the humans are," Stanley replied.

A low burp finally worked its way out of Richard, providing a small measure of relief. "So, what you're telling us is that there might be an unkillable monster hurting little kids. It could be Busar, or maybe not. No one knows for sure, and he's unkillable, too. Meanwhile, in order to get to the two immortals, we've got to navigate a rainforest full of spooks during a time when the leaders of the spooks might just have it out for us because you had a messy breakup with your girlfriend, The Devil. Assuming she's reassembled herself from the pile of ash you left her in, she might also be coming after us at any moment."

For the first time since they left the restaurant, Stanley reached for the cup of tea he'd ordered and took a long drink. After he set it back in the cup holder, he nodded. "I think you're starting to get the idea."

Burke retreated to her place next to Gordon.

"So, we're about as screwed as a port hooker the day after the navy docks," Richard muttered.

"Yes, about that screwed," Stanley agreed. He sipped his tea again. The little lines around his eyes scrunched like crepe paper as a smile crossed his face. "I'm glad you're all with me. I take great comfort in your presence."

Richard had been dying alone in a nursing home when Stanley found him. As far as he could figure, every day since then had been borrowed time, so what the heck. If a man had to go, he might as well go down in a blaze of glory. Thinking of it that way, Richard had to admit that he took great comfort in being part of their little posse too. Still, they'd be having a snowball fight in Hell before he admitted it out loud to Stanley freaking Kapcheck.